To Sail Atlantis

BY

Henry Hallan

Leabhar Cnoc Mhuilinn

For Kumar.

"So, then, the best of the historians is subject to the poet; for, whatsoever action or faction, whatsoever counsel, policy, or war-stratagem the historian is bound to recite, that may the poet, if he list, with his imitation, make his own, beautifying it both for further teaching, and more delighting, as it please him..."

- "The Defence of Poesy", Philip Sidney

$$-1-$$

The Scent of Orange Blossom

Once upon a time, in a corner of King Philip's Spain that I will not name, there lived a nobleman's son named Gustavo. His father had fought pagans in the New World and his grandfather had fought pagans with King Ferdinand. He grew up longing to match their acts of chivalry and strength of arms.

At the age of ten Gustavo's grandfather found for him a companion. He looked forward to a brother in arms, of course. So, when he learned that she was a girl, his disappointment was as bitter as his hope had been sweet. But Eva was not like a normal girl and, slowly, he came to appreciate her companionship.

Gustavo stood beneath her window and threw a stone. It rattled on the shutters. "Eva!" he called. "Come on, wake up!"

He was reaching for another stone when the shutters opened. "Gustavo," she called down, "Are you going to throw another rock? Why not pick that one? It's as big as your head and nearly as hard."

"I thought you'd fallen asleep."

"I've been awake for hours." She came out onto the balcony. She was a tall girl, as tall as Gustavo, with wild blonde hair and blue eyes like chips of heaven. She was dressed much as he was, in tunic, leggings and boots. Eva leaned over the balcony rail and put one leg over. Once she had found her footing on the outside of the balcony she put her other foot over and clambered down. He looked up, impressed with her agility and the strength in her legs and arms.

"Come on then," she said. "Don't stand there all morning with your mouth hanging open."

They half-crept, half-ran from the big house, under the orange trees and to the wall. She found the hole where the stream ran through in winter and

     To Sail Atlantis

she wriggled through. Gustavo was still struggling to catch up as she ran down the rough slope to the cold Atlantic. By the time he had caught her up she was in the water up to her knees. She kicked out at him, splashing him.

"Hey!" he shouted, "I thought you wanted to practice sword with me."

"Oh, you're no fun at all," she teased. But she waded back out of the water and together they found their cache of practice weaponry.

Theodosus saw the house perched on the hill, surrounded by the orange trees. He had been saving the horse but when he saw the gates he kicked his heels. They trotted up to the gate. The guard was an old man, half asleep, but he stood up when heard the hooves on the road. He looked up at Theodosus. "Welcome, father," he said.

He saw a rider with weather-lined face and iron-grey beard, wearing the habit of a monk. But beneath the rough black cloth he saw the hilt of a sword and the glitter of armour. He opened the gate and Theodosus rode in.

He found Gustavo out in front of the house, being taught riding. "Is that you, Gustavo?" he called. "You are much taller than you were when I was last here. But you need to keep your back straight."

Gustavo turned his horse's head and they walked over. "Father Theodosus," he replied, "Grandfather said you were coming to stay."

"And there is your grandfather now," Theodosus said, looking over at the house. He got down from the horse and they embraced.

Gustavo rode back to his tutor. "May I be excused?" he asked.

"Of course," his tutor replied. The tutor held the reins as he got down and ran over.

"I trust your journey was uneventful," Grandfather said to Theodosus.

"Have you forgotten our journeys, my friend? Do you remember those savages that attacked us in México? It is many years since we fought on that dreadful morning, but I remember that and I don't fear a few Spanish beggars."

"Of course not," agreed Grandfather.

"How are you? Are you well?"

"My eyesight is not what it was. And this knee–"

"This flesh is mortal, my friend."

"But we need to take care of it. Come inside." He raised his voice to call the servants. "Find breakfast. Find wine. Father Theodosus will want refreshments after his long journey."

* * *

So it was that Gustavo and Eva were sent to bed early, so their grandfather could talk with Father Theodosus and reminisce about their days in the lands of the heathen New World. They waited for the darkness and then Gustavo crept back to Eva's balcony.

Eva climbed down again. "I thought you would wake everyone," she whispered.

"I thought you would be ready to go," he countered.

"I had to get dressed," she replied. "Maria wouldn't leave. She talked and talked and in the end I had to tell her I wanted to sleep. She went on and on about dresses and dancing with boys: all kinds of things." Eva wrinkled her nose in disgust. "She tucked me into bed as if I was a child. I thought she'd never go. What a boring life ladies are expected to live!"

"What would you rather be?" Gustavo asked. This conversation was one they had held many times before.

"I'd like to be a conquistador and sail away to the New World. We could go together and face savages who would want to hack our still-living hearts from our bodies. But we'd fight them and win, and make them swear allegiance to King Philip and to Jesus Christ. Then we would bring home as much gold as our ships could carry."

"Well, let us learn about that, then."

Gustavo took her hand and together they crept along the walls. The shutters were open to let in the cool of the night and they could hear Grandfather talking. "... they are children, Theodosus. There is no impropriety."

"But they are not children anymore. They are a young man and woman, they are starting to feel love, and they should not be alone together. What will you do if she has his child? This is no peasant girl you can put away. She may be an orphan but she is of noble birth."

Gustavo was shocked and embarrassed. He looked around and saw that Eva's eyes were wide with horror. Both let go of the other's hand at the same time.

Father Theodosus went on, "She must come away. I will speak to some friends in Madrid and we will find somewhere for her in the Escorial. I think I can find something for her."

"She seems very young to be a lady at court," replied Grandfather. He hesitated, as if waiting for an answer, then suddenly he added, "I'm not sure her father would have wanted her at court. He always wanted her to live a more simple life. I think she would have been closer to his wishes if she became a nun, or a–"

His words were interrupted as Father Theodosus leaned suddenly out of the open window. They were caught in the light of the lantern.

The next morning Gustavo did not risk Eva's balcony. Instead he walked the beach alone, watching the restless waves throw themselves against the sand and then ebb away to nothing. He kicked the foam but it was not the same when he was alone. He threw stones and he practiced a few feints, lunges and parries, but his heart was not in it. He threw the practice weapons back into their cache and climbed up the hillside back to the house.

The servants brought breakfast but he was not hungry. Grandfather was not up and Father Theodosus had gone out, down to the village. Gustavo remembered how excited he had been only the day before. But nothing had turned out the way he had imagined.

Gustavo found Eva sitting on the bench, beneath the orange trees, looking out at the ocean. Maria sat with her, but they were not talking. Maria looked up as he came over.

"You may go," he told her.

"I am sorry, Don Gustavo," she said formally, "But I may not. Your grandfather told me that I was not to leave you two alone together." She was afraid and embarrassed, but Gustavo knew she would not disobey Grandfather's orders. Eva glared at her, making her feel more uncomfortable.

"Perhaps I could sit over there," she offered, "Where I can see you." She got up and sat a short distance away, watching them.

He sat down beside Eva and she took his hand. Then she hesitated a moment and she put her arms around him. Gustavo held her, his nostrils taking in the scent of the orange trees mixed with the scent of her hair. When they had held one another a while they parted a little. They lingered there a moment, her face was close to his, surrounding him with her golden hair and her breath. Blue eyes looked at his and for a moment he saw her fear.

"Is it true, then?" Gustavo asked.

"You fool," she laughed. "You really do have rocks in your head. Of course it is true. And you know it is true too, don't you?"

"I do," he admitted. "Why didn't you tell me before?"

"Why didn't *you* tell *me* before, Gustavo? It is your job. You are the man, after all."

"I... because I am a fool," he admitted. "Because I have rocks in my head."

Then she smiled at him and she was his childhood companion again. "I forgive you. My friend."

"So what now?"

"They mean me to go to King Philip's court," she said. "They'll make me behave like a courtly lady when I'd rather be a knight. But at least it's not a nunnery."

"The Escorial Palace is a monastery," Gustavo replied. "It's attached to one, anyway, which is nearly the same. You will be seeing plenty of monks and maybe nuns too. King Philip's father, old king Charles, was the Holy Roman Emperor. I guess that is why he is surrounded by the Church."

Eva shuddered. "I don't like nuns," she confided. "They make me feel..." she looked for words that could describe it without being blasphemous. "There's something not natural about them. They're like dried-up old things, old women who aren't anybody's grandmother. I'd hate to be one of them. How do you know they won't make me?"

"They won't, Evita."

"What are we going to do?" she whispered.

As suddenly as that Gustavo knew. "We will get married," he said.

Again she wrapped her arms around him, ignoring the expression of disapproval on Maria's face. "How will you marry me if I am in Madrid?" she asked.

"I will come to Madrid and marry you there. It won't be long before Grandfather will allow me to travel alone. You will wait for me, won't you?"

"Of course I will," she said. "I would wait for as long as you need."

"You won't need to wait long. And then, when we are married, nobody can keep us apart."

She pulled him close to her again. "I will wait for you, love," she whispered. "I will wait for you forever."

And so it was agreed. When Father Theodosus left for Madrid he took Eva and Maria. They followed the carriage with carts, carrying a vast amount of luggage. There were so many things Mother insisted Eva should take with her. Each time she said, "You cannot go to the Court without one of these."

But eventually the packing was over and they set out. Tears ran over Eva's cheeks and Gustavo's mother saw it and began to weep herself, although she was happy to see her adopted daughter going to the glories of King Philip's court. She thought Eva was feeling the same, but Gustavo knew what she really felt.

"Promise me you'll write," she whispered as he helped her into the carriage.

"Of course I will," he promised. "It won't be long before we are together."

The carriage rolled away and she waved at him out of the window. They went through the gateway and out into the road. Gustavo stood at the gate and watched the carriage and carts roll away, kicking up dust that he could see rising long after they had gone out of sight.

He wrote to her every day and, at first, her replies came often. But suddenly they stopped. He guessed she was busy but he wrote anyway. He did not allow himself to think of the alternatives.

"*Dona* Eva," her secretary said. "There is another of those letters for you."

"Thank you, Antonio," she replied. "I need something to make me laugh."

"It's in your writing desk, Our Lady," he said as he shuffled out.

She sat down with a glass of wine and broke the seal. The handwriting had improved over the last three years: a childish hand had become a firm script.

> *My dear Evita,*
> *I know you have not replied to one of my letters for more than two years but I have not forgotten you. Grandfather has agreed that I should go on tour and, accordingly, he has arranged for me to travel to Madrid before going on to Barcelona and then by ship to Rome.*
> *I understand that perhaps your heart has grown cold towards me and that you have not written because you do not wish to disappoint me, but I must know. If you have found someone else I will understand.*
> *But if you still love me, as I hope and pray that you do, then we can finally be together.*

> *Rest assured though, I will take no for an answer. However, I*
> *find that I must have an answer.*
> *With all my love,*
> *Gustavo.*

"Does he still amuse you?" Antonio asked.

"This is perhaps a little more serious." She dropped the letter on the writing desk and got up. "Speak to Luisa and tell her that I need her to pack. We are going on a journey."

"Where are we going?" Antonio asked. Eva knew that he didn't like to leave the monastery.

"We are going to pay the young Don Gustavo a little visit."

"Very good, Our Lady. Is this purely a visit for sport?"

"Not purely. He could be a threat. I think we must travel with the Inquisition."

"I am sure they will find plenty to do out in the countryside, Dona Eva."

"I am sure they will. I keep hearing rumours that the Midsummer Children dare to live there."

"It is a while since we have seen them, Our Lady."

"Time we looked more carefully, then."

"As you wish, Our Lady. I will inform Father Theodosus."

Gustavo had been out riding along the beach, following the paths that he used to ride with Evita. He had got out of the habit of thinking of her. Or rather he had learned to force himself not to think of her. When he had thought of her and how she no longer replied to his letters, just getting through the simplest daily chores had become unbearable. So he had not thought of her for a long time.

But now, knowing that he would see her in Madrid in a few weeks, he was able to think of her again. Instead of facing despair he felt hope rise in his heart when he rode the paths they had ridden together. He imagined how she might be, of what might have trapped her and prevented her from replying, and he imagined how he would rescue her and they would ride back here, to his grandfather's house, to live the rest of their lives in happiness.

As the horse found its way back through the orange trees, white with blossom, Gustavo saw some sort of commotion around the stables. A rich coach was there, shining in the Sun, surrounded by men-at-arms and accompanied by two cartloads of luggage. Servants were unloading the carts and taking care of the horses. Some of them were his grandfather's servants but most of them were strangers.

He rode up to the stable doors. One of his grandfather's lads hurried over to take the horse's head. "Don Gustavo!" he exclaimed, "She is here! She has returned!"

"Who?" Gustavo demanded as he jumped down.

"Dona Eva, lord," he replied.

"With all this entourage? Who is she travelling with?" he asked. He felt a sudden pang of fear in his chest. "Has she found some rich man to take care of her?"

"No, my lord," the stable-hand replied. "These things are all hers. She is dressed as a single woman, she has men-at-arms, she has ladies-in-waiting. Father Theodosus came with her, my lord, and he has taken a vow of poverty." The stable-hand leaned closer. "I think they might be the Inquisition, Don Gustavo."

"Well, the Inquisition will have plenty to do," Gustavo replied. "There is too much superstition in the village."

Gustavo saw the fear on his face as the stable-hand crossed himself. "I am sure you are right, my lord."

Gustavo dismissed him and went inside. He heard Grandfather talking and he recognised Father Theodosus replying. Then he heard a woman's laughter, a girlish sound that sent a thrill through him. Could that really be his Eva? He took a deep breath and opened the door.

They stopped speaking and looked around. She was wearing a blue dress made of shimmering silk, that reflected every colour of the sea as the fabric turned. Every other woman Gustavo had seen dressed in dark colours, predominantly black. He knew he was taller than he had been but she was as tall as him, standing taller than Father Theodosus and much taller than Grandfather. She looked straight at him. For a moment her face was a perfectly sculptured mask framed by curly hair the colour of honey, but it seemed that the coldness of her blue-green eyes was the ruthless inhumanity of a snake, an eagle or a shark. His heart skipped a beat and then she smiled. She ran over just like the girl he remembered. She took his fingers in her hands.

"You have grown, Gustavo," she said. Her accent had changed in three years of court life. "Come and walk with me."

His throat was too tight for words, but somehow he found his voice. "Where do you want to go?" he croaked.

"Show me how things have changed," she answered.

He turned to lead her out, but behind him Theodosus began to speak. "Are you sure that..?"

She turned to Theodosus. "Do you dare?" she snapped.

"Of course you must do what you think is wisest, Our Lady," he replied. Gustavo was shocked to see how a brave man could be reduced to so little by three words from a girl of his own age.

"I will do as I please, Theodosus. Wisdom be damned." She turned back to Gustavo with a smile. "Come on, my love."

He led her out and under the orange groves. "Did you..?" he began. "Did you receive my letters?"

"Every one," she replied.

"Why have you not replied for so long?"

"I will explain that later," she answered. "There is a perfectly simple explanation and you will understand right away. But for now I want you to show me."

"What do you want to see?"

"Show me everything. Show me the places you have treasured in your heart for the last three years."

He led her down to the beach. "Remember this?" he asked her, as he moved the rocks aside. The wooden swords were still there. "Remember?"

"Show me," she replied.

"You want to practice sword?" he asked. "How could you practice sword wearing a dress?"

"If I solve that problem will you try?"

"Of course," he answered. "But I wouldn't wish to have an advantage."

"You won't have an advantage," she smiled.

He gathered up the swords. When he turned back she was lifting the dress over her head. "Help me with this, will you?" she asked. She hitched the petticoat up above her knees and tied it. His mouth went dry as he saw the shape of her body inside the thin silk. He glanced up the rocks but nobody was watching.

"How do you dare?" he whispered.

"I dare anything I want," she replied. "Do you want me to marry you, Don Gustavo?"

"I... I mean, we promised–"

"If you can beat me with the sword, Don Gustavo, then I will marry you."

"Very well," he replied. He offered her one of the wooden swords. She took it and weighed it in her hand a moment. Then she turned to him and he bowed. She raised the point of her wooden sword high and touched the hilt to her forehead. He raised the wooden blade ready to make defence. She didn't seem to be trying at all. He lunged.

She batted the wooden blade away and laughed. "Wait a moment, Gustavo. We have not said what will happen if I beat you."

He smiled nervously. "What do you want?"

"I want you. If I beat you then I will own you, Don Gustavo. You will be my plaything until I am bored of you."

"But if I beat you then you will marry me?"

"That is correct. Will you play my game?"

"Yes, my dear Evita."

"Then begin."

Gustavo looked at her. Her beauty, her breathtaking flesh under the silk was distracting him, but she seemed to have forgotten everything he had taught her. Her sword was not up, defending her and keeping him away. Instead the point hung down, trailing on the sand by her foot. He stepped into a lunge aiming at her shoulder.

She stepped slightly out of the way and he missed her. Wordlessly he cursed himself for allowing his mind to wander. He held the blade before her and swept it slightly, aiming for the side of her neck just below her jawline. He saw her earrings on her skin as she turned, beautiful turquoise beads among the cascade of her curls. He felt a shock in his fingers as she beat his blade down and turned to find her blade in his face, pointed just below his chin.

"You are toying with me," she laughed. "Come on, if you really want me."

He stepped back and looked at her. She still wasn't making much effort to defend herself, so he lunged again. This time her blade did touch his, just for a moment, then she stepped beside him. One foot hooked his ankle and she pushed his shoulder. He sprawled on the sand. As he turned over she put her boot on his chest. He looked up along the blade of her sword.

"You have been learning in Madrid," he said. "It is a style I do not recognise. You should teach me."

"Why should I?" she asked. "You are my plaything." She sat down heavily on him, landing on his hip and stomach and knocking the wind out of him. He feebly raised the sword but she twisted it out of his hand and threw it away. She leaned over him and he looked into her blue-green eyes as her weight shifted in his lap. her hair fell forward, surrounding him with the fragrance of her, and her breath caught in his nostrils...

He put up his hands to push her away. The scent of his Eva was something he knew he would never forget, an unspoken language of love.

He pushed her shoulders hard enough that he could see into her face. "You are not my Eva," he said.

He saw disappointment in the pout of her mouth. "Oh, that is a pity!" she exclaimed. "I hoped there would be better sport."

"Who are you?" he demanded. Then, as his mind caught up, he added, "What have you done with my Eva?"

"Of course I am not your Eva," she agreed as she stood up. "Theodosus brought her to me because the resemblance was strong."

Gustavo struggled to his feet. "What have you done with her?" he demanded.

"What do you think I have done with her? I needed her face and her name. Theodosus assured me she was an orphan. We didn't expect your letters."

"Father Theodosus? He is a friend of our family! How could he betray us?"

"He is a friend of your grandfather, Gustavo. But why would he care about some orphan girl that his friend's son's wife took in?"

"Did you hurt her?"

"Of course I didn't hurt her. She had done me no harm. Why would I hurt her?"

"Then she is still alive?" Gustavo began to hope. "I am going on a Grand Tour. If you give her to me I will take her far away. You will never see her again."

"I will never see her again anyway," she told him. "Every so often I need to die. Who do you think was in my coffin at my last funeral?"

"You murdered her?" Gustavo demanded. He drew his sword in one angry movement. "You murdered my Eva?"

"Of course I did," she replied.

Gustavo noticed that she was carrying herself with the same relaxed posture that she had used when they had been fighting with wooden swords. But this time she had no weapon. He raised the point of the blade to her face. "You will not get away with this," he told her.

The movement took him by surprise, but he felt the blow in his hand. The sword in his hand snapped like a twig, leaving him with no more than a hands-width of blade poking out of the basket. In her hand was a sword, flat-bladed, single-edged and as long as her arm. It had cut through the fine Toledo steel as if it were no more than a green stick. He had no idea where she had found the weapon.

"I will get away with this," she told him. "I have got away with it hundreds of times before and I will get away with it hundreds of times more. I have lived more than six thousand years, through Rome and Egypt before it. You are not going on any Grand Tour, Gustavo. Your Eva's death was quick and painless, but yours will be anything but. You will confess to the Inquisition and then you will burn as an unrepentant heretic."

"What do I have to confess?" he answered.

"Anything they want you to confess," she breathed. "The Inquisition know their work. When they are done with you, you will confess whatever we tell you to confess. Many are more brave than you, but when they are finished they are all frightened children crying for their daddy. And there is never a daddy to make it better."

"We have a Father in Heaven, witch. And you will have to face judgement one day."

"That is where you are wrong. There is no God. I know it to be true and so do the priests who will oversee your confession. God is a fable we use to keep you peasants in check." She looked beyond him and he turned to see. She threw her strange sword out and into the sea. He looked around just as his Grandfather and Father Theodosus hurried down.

"Oh Grandfather," she exclaimed, holding her arms over her body in a pretence of modesty, "Thank the Virgin that you are here! It was horrible. He attacked me and forced me to take off my dress. If he hadn't broken his sword, I don't know what he would have made me do."

— 2 —

A Flight from Flames

A knight falls from the Starry River
Takes the token of a virgin queen
Folly frees old Neptune's secrets
Never more will they be seen

The young man put the writing back on the desk, as if he had no further wish to touch it. He was thin with brown eyes and a shock of light brown hair. He looked at the older man for approval after bringing such a piece of treason.

The older man smiled. He was in his fifties, with a softly-forked white beard and blue eyes that could easily be called "kindly". But the young man knew that he would be anything but kindly where the enemies of England were concerned.

"Philip," the older man asked, "Are you sure this comes from Doctor Dee's pen?"

"He read it to me himself, Lord Burghley," Philip replied. "I copied it down as soon as I could but I cannot guarantee every word is in place."

"I understand," Burghley replied. "But your tutors at Oxford praised your ability with words and poetry, Philip. I am sure you are capable of remembering a simple piece of doggerel such as that."

"I am sure about some of the words. The knight definitely takes the token of a virgin queen, my lord."

"And did Doctor Dee explain how he came by this verse?"

"He said it was dictated by angels."

"I will believe it when an angel brings it to me," Burghley snorted. "Not before."

"Why do you think he wrote it, my lord?" Philip asked. "It seems like such a risk."

"It is a risk. Did he mention what was going on after the treaty that was signed this spring?"

19

"Treaty, my lord?"

"Her Majesty signed a treaty with Catherine de Medici, the Regent of France, agreeing to forget our differences and unite to oppose Spain."

"I don't understand how that relates."

"That is because you don't understand what happened with the treaty. The de Medicis would very much like to arrange a marriage between Her Majesty and one of their sons. I don't quite see how the House of Valois links with this 'Starry River', but if the link could be made–"

"I see. I think Doctor Dee suggested the constellation of the River, that flows from the Water Carrier's jar. But much of Doctor Dee's science is too subtle for me."

"The Latin word for witchcraft means wickedness and, in my experience, a lot of what passes for witchcraft and divination is actually treasonous thoughts wrapped in a package of mystery. We shall have to watch your friend Doctor Dee very carefully."

"As you wish, my lord," Philip replied.

They locked Gustavo in the church tower, to await the Inquisition. They started with the people of low birth; an old woman who lived apart from the village, known for her healing powers and for the oddness of her life. Many consulted with her, but in secret. None were really her friends.

"I don't need friends from the village," she would say. "The woods have all the friends I need."

Having no friends meant there was nobody to speak up for her when the Inquisition called. They asked her lots of questions and she laughed at them. Then she escaped and, a few hours later, with great excitement, they caught her again. The manner of her escape was a mystery to the whole village: but something about her escape or her recapture encouraged the Inquisition. They asked her their questions again, but this time with strappado and upon the rack. This time she did not laugh.

The priests led out the old woman and Gustavo watched them mouthing the pieties that he now knew they did not believe. The old woman was tied to the prepared stake and two sacks were thrown on the pyre. The two sacks were lumpy and heavy and they seemed to stir slightly as they landed on the heaped wood.

"Her imps will be burned with her," announced Father Theodosus as they were heaved up.

Then they turned the garrotte and the old woman started to strangle. Her eyes bulged and Gustavo saw the terror on her face as the executioner completed his grim work. Then they withdrew and set light to it all. Gustavo watched as the flames roared and the bundles struggled. He realised that the bags must contain her pets.

As he watched this spectacle Gustavo heard a child crying, despair in her voice that sounded like it would never be consoled. At first it seemed to him as if his heart had found a voice of its own, realising the years his love had laid in her borrowed grave, with no one to mourn her. But now he was going to die. He felt he should have composed his soul to meet his Maker, but all he could think of was the witch who had taken his beloved's face and name. All he could remember was her blasphemy – blasphemy from someone who arrived at the head of the Inquisition.

He felt a tug at his sleeve. "You are Don Gustavo?" a child's voice beside him asked. "Don Gustavo from the big house? What are you doing here? What did they accuse you of?"

He glanced up. In the instant he turned he saw a shy little child, with blue eyes and long, straggly hair the colour of straw. Her hair curled up at the ends, giving her a pronounced fringe. He saw the redness around her eyes and the tear-streaks on her cheeks. He turned away again. "What do you want?" he asked, not caring.

"What are you doing here? Have the Inquisition accused you too?"

"What do you think?" he asked bitterly, not looking back at her.

"How do they dare?" she asked. "Surely your grandfather would–"

"My grandfather would not dare oppose the Inquisition."

"Don Gustavo, you are being naive. Your grandfather could bribe the bishop and they would–"

"They are not led by a bishop," Gustavo grumbled. "They are led by... an immortal witch."

"*Oh my...*" began the girl. "*She* is here? She will kill us all, Don Gustavo. You have to get away."

"How can I get away? Where would I go?" He sighed. "And why would I bother? Soon I will be with my beloved in Heaven."

"Are you sure?" she asked. "Do you think you will be allowed into Heaven when you have let that... witch have her way with everyone?"

"How can I save them? I cannot even save myself."

"Your father was a brave man, Don Gustavo. You can save yourself with a little help. And you can save me too. Save me and I will help you have revenge on her."

"I cannot unlock the door," he told her.

"I will unlock the door," she told him. "But I cannot ride and I cannot travel the roads. The Inquisition would find me and kill me."

"Because you are a witch?"

"Because she hates me. She hates all my people. If she finds us she will kill us."

Gustavo said nothing.

"I know you are upset," she said. "I'm upset too. That was my family they burned down there, Don Gustavo. But we have to go. There will be time enough to grieve later."

"I will grieve for the rest of my life," he told her.

"As will I. But now we need to escape. If I open the door will you take me with you?"

He sighed. "Very well. Open the door and I will take you to safety."

"Do you promise?"

"I am a man of my word," he told her.

He didn't see what she did next. He expected to hear a sound from the door but instead he heard the shutters of the window move. Then it was silent and he wondered if she was still there. Just as he was thinking he would look up to check, he heard the bolt drawn on the door. He looked around. She had to force the door open with her shoulder.

For the first time he saw the shape of her body. "What are you?" he demanded. "Are you a demon?"

"I am as human as you are," she snapped. "Now, are you a man of your word or not?"

He remembered the many tales he had heard of men tricked by imps or demons. But what else could he do? He took his sword then followed her as she slipped out. The stairway was empty. For ten anxious breaths he ran down the stairs on his toes, hoping nobody would hear his feet on the stone. He crept out of the church and into a stable behind it. There were horses in the stable and he flung on saddle and bridle as quickly as he could. The spectacle of what the Inquisition were doing outside was enough to distract attention away from his departure. With the whole town out enjoying the entertainment, he encountered nobody as he led his horse out of the stable and away from the village.

He lifted her into the saddle in front of him, like a child. It was difficult and, after a bit of struggle, they found that she sat much more comfortably behind him, clinging to his back with her arms around him and her fingers clutching at his shirt. She was so short he could fit her under his cloak. Her grip was tight like a baby.

When they had ridden away from the town, he asked her, "Where are we going?"

"Somewhere where I am safe," she replied. "Outside the domain of the Inquisition."

"North or South, then?" he asked "Protestant, or Moor?"

"My grandmother told me about the Moors. Your grandfather fought against them. The Protestants at least believe in Jesus Christ," she replied. "Let us go north."

Gustavo turned the horse's head towards the northern road. As he did he wondered how a demon could use the name of Jesus. "Do you know you still haven't told me your name," he told her.

"I am Madimi."

They rode north.

He had been in the saddle a long time, but the young man still rode without slouching. Ahead of him was the Solent, stretching away southwards to the sea, with the Isle of Wight a blue shadow on the horizon, outlined by the vivid white cliffs. Where the land met the sea a few houses gathered together. They were Southampton: Christopher Stoke's destination.

The people of Southampton were used to the comings and goings of strangers. This stranger rode confidently, sitting up tall in the saddle as the horse trotted. Saddlebags were full and his clothing carried some of the showiness of a merchant's son: delicate lace for his ruff, fine velvet and a feather for his cap, gold brocade for his jerkin and fur at his shoulder, trimming his cloak.

At the waterfront he called down to one of the men working, repairing nets. "Good afternoon," Christopher called. "I am looking for Edward Horsey."

"Edward Horsey is Governor of the Isle of Wight, sir," the man replied.

"But that is his boat over there, is it not?"

The man turned around to look. The boat was the *Dragonfly*, a merchant barque of no more than a hundred tons. The crew and shore-men were unloading a cargo of something that was contained in barrels. The man called out. "John," he shouted, "There's a fellow here who is looking for Edward."

The big man who was supervising the loading got up and came over. He was not just tall, but powerfully built, with his muscular frame squeezed into a leather jerkin. The sword he wore was simple and functional, but the confidence this John carried in his movements suggested he would rarely need to use it. "Who are you?" he asked.

"I am Christopher Stoke. I was told that Edward Horsey needed a surgeon for a voyage."

"I think he might. Our previous surgeon took a fancy to a girl and gave up the sea. It is not unusual. A good voyage can set a man up for life.

And the last three voyages have been good. Captain Ranse does not take wild risks, but he finds enough Spanish gold for everyone."

"Perhaps there will be enough for me, then."

"That is not my decision to make. I will take you to Edward Horsey." John walked down the gangplank among the men carrying barrels and led Christopher into an inn. As Christopher led his horse away he thought he could hear the man who was mending nets laugh at him. But he focused on following John Overy.

John led them to an inn and Christopher tied the horse outside before he followed. He found John's bulky shape in the smoky darkness and followed a while before John turned towards a table. The three men drinking were rough sorts of gentlemen, their clothes expensive but their chins stubbly. Christopher tagged them in his mind according to the showiness of their dress. The one who spoke first was the one whose dress was most conservative. Christopher thought back to what he knew of Sixteenth Century menswear: this man's dark, undecorated clothes suggested puritan, but his presence in an inn did not fit with that suggestion.

"Is the boat unloaded yet?" perhaps-puritan asked.

"No, Captain," John replied. "But this gentleman said that he had heard that the *Dragonfly* needs a surgeon."

It was not the puritanical captain that replied, nor the man with the richest clothes. "Where did you study medicine, then?"

"Oxford," Christopher replied. "I brought letters of recommendation."

"Good. I am Horsey and the *Dragonfly* is mine. At least I pay the bills and occasionally turn a profit by her voyages. The true master is James here. If your letters of recommendation are good then I will say yes, but it is James that you have to convince."

Christopher looked at James Ranse and relaxed his face into an open, honest smile. "I have never lost a patient yet," he said.

"Well if you sail with us you will lose plenty," Ranse growled. "Last voyage we set off with fifty-two men and returned with twenty-three. The fortunes of those two dozen men are assured, but less than half survived. That is a voyage upon which Fortune smiled."

"How did they die?"

"Three died in fights, two with the Spanish and one with another crew member. One drowned, one was struck by an un-stayed spar and one died in his sleep, nobody knows why. The others all died of agues, fluxes and bad beer. The air of Hispaniola is loaded with bad miasmas and of course breathing it gives ague. And the water and heat give fluxes too. A man can die between sunrise and sunset if he gets a bad flux."

"What did your surgeon recommend?"

"Poppy resin," Ranse replied.

"That would stop the flux, but the side-effects are... inconvenient."

"What would you recommend?"

"I would give the patient a drink made of one part sea-water to twelve parts fresh water, boiled, cooled and sweetened with two ounces of honey to every pint. It is not the flux that kills, it is the weakness that comes from not being able to keep food and water inside. But I prefer prevention to cure. Fluxes may be prevented by making sure that food, water and the hands that prepare them are clean. And the agues that come from the tropical forests may be prevented by good curtains. A fine muslin cloth enables the air to circulate but prevents the disease-causing agent from passing through."

"Well, that is an interesting theory."

"I hope to demonstrate to you that it is more than theory," Stoke replied.

Ranse looked at Horsey and Horsey shrugged. "One voyage," Ranse said. "But if you cannot set a bone or stitch a wound, I will throw you overboard."

"You won't have to," Stoke replied. "And one voyage will be all I need."

Hasten out to patch the Camick
Besieged by youths, old king now meek
Invisible, within the mountains
The priestess urges them to seek

John Dee looked up from his writing and sighed, "When the angels give you a verse like that, I can almost feel the hangman's noose tighten around my neck. What is all this talk of invisibility and priestesses? You know how people feel about witchcraft."

"We are doing God's work, Doctor," Barnabas replied. "But God's ways are mysterious."

Dee put down the quill. He was an old man now, in his mid-forties, with grey hair under a velvet skull-cap. He was dressed in clothes that were rich and well-made but understated. His companion was a younger man, a farmer's son from East Anglia. Dee leaned over his writing desk and Barnabas peered into the crystal. The smoke from the incense curled around Barnabas Saul's head, stirred into turbulence by the draught from the candle flames.

"I see the angel!" he exclaimed.

Dee picked up his quill and waited. Then he looked up. Barnabas had gone quiet. "What is the matter, man?" he asked.

"I see the angel," Barnabas repeated. "She is standing inside the doorway." He was staring through the open door into the hall. Dee realised he was very afraid. Then they heard a high-pitched voice, like that of a child, speaking Latin.

"*I have brought a knight to your house,*" the voice said.

"I hear her!" exclaimed Dee. Then he realised that Barnabas had not understood. "*Where is this knight, then?*" he asked.

"*He is outside. Open your front door and let him in. You must help him. The angels command it.*"

Dee hurried to the door and unbolted it, not sure what to expect. He held up his lantern and a face appeared out of the darkness. "*Hello knight,*" he called, in Latin.

Don Gustavo stepped into the light and his host opened the door wide to let him in.

Once inside, Don Gustavo was led to the table where a cold meal was laid out. There was beef, bacon and mutton, and sweets of various sorts. The man of the house introduced himself. "I am Doctor John Dee, and I am astrologer to the Court." He indicated his assistant. "This is Barnabas Saul, who has the second sight. It is he who saw the angel that announced your presence."

Don Gustavo couldn't see Madimi, but he guessed that she was helping herself to beef, bacon and mutton and sweets of various sorts. Her appetite was as small as the rest of her and nobody ever noticed.

He replied, "My name is Gustavo. I am from Spain, but I was forced to flee by a witch who controls the Inquisition. Madimi heard your name in Antwerp, at the Sign of the Golden Angel in the Kammerstraat, and we decided to come here. They told us you were a great magician. I have met a great magician, and she has done me wrong. Perhaps you could help me to get my vengeance."

Mention of a magician immediately gained Dee's attention. "This great magician? What is his name?"

"The name she uses is Eva. But her name is stolen. It was stolen from my betrothed. To steal her name the witch also stole her life." Don Gustavo sighed, but in anger or in sorrow, Dee could not tell. "She told me that this is something she does – she finds a young woman who resembles her, kills her, and then takes her place. If the girl who is murdered has newly arrived at court, nobody will notice the deception. My beloved Evita was chosen because she was an orphan and the witch thought that she had no loved ones to notice. But my Evita had family: she had me. We were betrothed in secret. The witch avoided me for years but eventually we met and I knew straight away. For that, the Inquisition have sentenced me to a heretic's death."

Dee shuddered at mention of a heretic's death. He said, "How do you know that she is what she claims to be?"

"Since we know she is an immortal, we can see her appearance in other places. Madimi knows who she has pretended to be since before King Ferdinand was on the throne. She has been at the Court of the Holy Roman Emperor since the days of Charlemagne, close to the source of power: back to the reign of the Emperor Constantine – and before."

"You know that your King Philip is not the Holy Roman Emperor?" Dee smiled at the humour of it. "You know that his cousin Maximilian of Bohemia has taken it from him? And that he is Lutherian?"

"They don't teach that to Spanish children," replied Gustavo, "Although I heard it at the Sign of the Golden Angel. It is the Protestant monarchs that are resisting her. But do not underestimate her, doctor. She made herself Queen Isabella's favourite so she could conquer the wealth of the New World. Everything she has done since she came to Spain has been making Spain strong, which is bad for Spain's enemies, like England."

"Why is England her enemy? Other than the enemy of all Spanish, that is?"

"You don't understand. She is not Spanish. She is older than Spain. Madimi says she is from Atlantis, the island that Solon learned about from the Egyptians, thousands of years old when their Greek civilisation was young. She is older than Christianity, older than the Greeks, as old as the Flood. For surely the Flood of Noah is the same event as the destruction of Atlantis told in Plato's account. England is her enemy because England steals the treasures of the New World. The gold is melted down, but every jewel from the New World is property of King Philip and taken to the Escorial Palace for her to see. There is something, some golden prize in those treasures that she wants. And, if she wants it, I want to take it from her."

"Then you have come to the right place, Don Gustavo. Here in England there are many people who will help thwart this evil witch's plans."

"There is a letter for you, Our Lady."

The woman who called herself Eva turned to her assistant. "Where is it, Antonio?"

"I put it on your desk, Our Lady."

"Who is it from?"

"Don Guerau de Espés, Our Lady. He writes in Latin–"

Eva sighed. "No doubt never using a word when a dozen will do." She broke the seal and skimmed the writing.

> *I am writing to you because I have news from my spies in England. As you know my circle has been reduced, but there are a few who are loyal to our king and our church. One of them has written to me with a worrying report.*

She skipped over his complaints about the English court and about how under-provisioned he was, eventually finding the report itself.

> *It appears that the Court Magician – I shudder to write of such a thing, but the Tudor court is not a God-fearing place – has taken in a certain young man from Spain. This young man has visited certain other courtiers seeking support for a venture to the New World. There is talk of some golden treasure. And, although I cannot put my finger on the reason for the suspicion, I suspect that you play a part in their plans, Our Lady.*

She flipped through the rest but it was only valedictions and flattery. She put the letter down.

"It's not good news, Our Lady?" Antonio asked.

"We may be running out of time," she replied. "After that incompetent Francisco let that peasant king escape before he gave up his secrets the search seems to have stalled. And now there is talk that the English court is sending a mission to find the Golden One."

"Our Lady, we have had so much gold and such treasure from the New World already. What difference can one more thing make?"

"You fool!" she snarled, "The City fell because the greatest treasure, the greatest power was lost. One traitor took it from our king and the City was gone in a day and night. He went eastwards but the weather forced us westwards. I have worked six thousand years to build a fleet strong enough to go back and take it by force. I expected to find an empire but instead I found two. Francisco told me that he was sure the king knew what we were looking for but still he let the king escape. It is my fault for trusting the matter to peasants."

"What else can you do, Our Lady?"

"I can go and see to this myself."

"But, Dona Eva, His Majesty has forbidden any Spanish woman to take ship for the New World without her husband."

"Don't you think I don't know that?"

"Then what will you do? Will you marry?"

"Don't you remember last time?" She sighed. "Of course you don't: it was nearly twenty years ago. Nearly fifty years running Spain from a widow's cell in a nunnery. When I have it in my hand things are going to change. So many things will change. When they see one of us in her full power, the kings of Europe will prostrate themselves in fear before me."

"Then you will wait until–"

"I will not wait any longer, Antonio. I will not wait for a man who dares to pretend to be my husband, nor for leave to sail from a monarch who daren't look me in the eye. Tell them all to prepare to sail. We will see this Francisco de Toledo and he can explain to me face-to-face why I placed any trust in him at all."

"But the king's orders–"

"He is not my king, Antonio. He is my servant as much as you are. If he has sense he will not draw attention to my going. If he opposes me then Spain will have a new king. I am bored of this now. Pack the household and find me a ship. We are going to the New World."

— 3 —

The Golden One

"Show them in, Philip" he said. Philip was there as another pair of eyes and ears. Everyone knew about Philip's achievements on the field of gold, but few knew what Burghley knew: that he was quick-witted, loyal to his country and his faith, brave, and a shrewd judge of character beyond his few years.

Dee was his usual self: with the outward appearance of a scholar but behind that the wheedling of a man who wished to turn the Queen's friendship into his fortune, or at least his living. Burghley did not recognise his companion. He was a younger man, perhaps as young as Philip, and he had the carriage of a soldier. He also had the dark looks of a Spaniard.

Dee made the introductions. "My Lord, Philip, this is Don Gustavo de Flores. Don Gustavo, this is Lord Burghley and Philip Sidney." Burghley noted the name of the strange young man. "Don Gustavo brings us news from Spain that we cannot ignore."

The two guests spoke well enough and Burghley saw that the young Spaniard was at least trained in politeness. Beneath the formality of a Spanish nobleman, Burghley could see anger and the pain that caused it. Don Gustavo put his hand in his tunic and brought out a page. On it was drawn a woman, an attractive face with high cheekbones, a rather flattened nose and pale curly hair over her shoulders. He dropped it on the desk in front of Burghley and began to tell his tale.

"I do not know the customs of England, but in Spain the children of nobility often play and grow together from an early age. Fortune and the whims of politics choose the companions for children who know nothing of either of these false friends, so we grow up with the companions that are chosen for us. Some are fortunate, some are less fortunate. Some gain power and influence through these allegiances and a few, the lucky ones, gain love. I was more fortunate than any man could ever wish. I was brought up in the company of this lady, Eva de Castilla, the most beautiful woman since Helen of Troy."

31

Burghley thought for a moment. Eva de Castilla was a name that he knew, but he could not remember much more about her than her name. He thought she might have some connection to the feud currently splitting the House of Hapsburg: but perhaps this was merely because that particular feud had been on his mind a lot recently. Certainly though, she wasn't heir to any important title or estate. He glanced down at the drawing and noted the name down to remember later. Don Gustavo continued his tale.

"We were supposed to grow together like brother and sister, or like cousins, but the plans of Venus were otherwise. We fell in love without telling anyone and we were secretly betrothed before we were parted. She went to Madrid, to serve in the Court, and we wrote to each other in our absence." Burghley, a skilled reader of gesture and intonation, could see the young man's anger and grief moving, a vague but monstrous shadow beneath the thin ice of his controlled soldier's exterior.

"One day, the letters stopped.

"At first, I did not understand. I could not imagine what I had done to cause offence. I wrote to her, letter after letter, asking her what had gone wrong and what could be done to make things right between us. But she never replied, not for months. Finally, I got my grandfather's permission to go to Madrid and I wrote to her to advise her of my plans. But she came to me first, with a group of churchmen. The churchmen were Inquisition and they were scouring the countryside of witches and demonologists." Dee looked uncomfortable, noted Burghley, but that was to be expected from a man like him – especially one who had survived Mary's reign.

Gustavo carried on. "When I met her, I realised what had happened. She was not my betrothed. She was someone who looked like her, true enough, and dressed as she was in the fashions of the court, I'm sure my grandfather never noticed. But I did. She told me what happened to my betrothed."

Burghley looked sceptical. "What had happened, then?"

"She was murdered. The woman you call Eva de Castilla is an immortal witch who steals the bodies of people who resemble her and takes their place. She is a survivor of Atlantis, from before the Flood. She rules Spain from the shadows. She is their kingmaker."

"How do you know this?"

"An angel told me," replied Gustavo with confidence. "The Inquisition was to burn me for heresy before I could accuse her. But a little angel freed me. The knowledge of Atlantis was passed down her family and she was able to explain these things to me."

Burghley looked at Dee. "Did you see this angel?"

"No."

"But then you never do." Dee looked uncomfortable, and Burghley turned to Gustavo. "Well, Don Gustavo, your tale has been most interesting. Thank you for telling it. Unfortunately, I am a busy man and I must turn my mind to affairs of state."

They left. As they were going, Burghley made one last barb. "Doctor Dee, pass on my greeting to Mr Saul. We always take an interest in his doings." He looked John Dee in the eye, waited a moment to be sure he understood the warning. "We take a keen interest, doctor."

The door closed behind them.

"You see?" said Burghley to Sidney. "This talk of angels spreads dismay among Her Majesty's subjects. Any spy from Spain arrives bearing such a tale and Doctor Dee will be instantly convinced. This seer of his, Master Saul, has a good line in such chicanery. Now the Spanish are sending spies to exploit this weakness." He sighed. "Most of the warrants that kill traitors are punishing folly, rather than malice. But folly seems to be unending in its supply."

"It is a fine story, though," replied Philip. "And that Spaniard's heart has been broken by something." Burghley saw something else in his young companion too: his curiosity had been aroused by tales of Atlantis.

"Broken hearts do not make for wise counsel, Philip. The folly that comes from a broken heart serves nobody, least the bearer of that burden."

He looked down at the woman in the drawing. The artist had only modest skill, but he had drawn his subject with obsessive detail.

"Where do you want it?" the voice cried out from the wharf.

John Overy wiped his face and stood up. Below him on the cobbles stood a hay-cart loaded with barrels. It was drawn by two oxen and a man stood by their heads. He looked up at John.

"What is this?" John demanded.

"Cider, sir," the man called back. "Your man ordered it. Ten shillings a barrel, he said."

"Where did you find cider this late in the summer?"

"It was hard enough to find, sir," the man replied. "We have scoured every cellar from here to Christchurch."

"What is wrong with honest beer?"

"I surely don't know. Ask your man Christopher. He was most insistent."

Just then Christopher came out of the inn. "What is this?" John demanded.

"And a very good morning to you, John," Christopher laughed back. "There is a goodness in apples that will prevent scurvy. The fermentation preserves the apples and the goodness will preserve your crew."

"Well, I am glad this is coming out of Master Horsey's purse and not mine." John turned away to the crew. "Get those barrels on board and stowed!" he called. He walked aft as the men got up and found the Captain's cabin.

Captain Ranse was already on his feet when John swept aside the muslin curtain and opened the door. "What is it now, John?" he asked.

"Cider," replied John.

Ranse looked at the curtain in his hand. "More crazy ideas."

"It is book learning that does it," John replied. "They stuff a doctor's head with such nonsense, Greek and Latin and stuff, that he can't hardly think about the simple cures we all know."

"There is only one book a man needs to read," agreed Ranse. "Still, nothing he has ordered is actually harmful. The men might not like a ration of cider instead of beer, but I am sure it will do them no harm."

"No harm other than it being twice the price, of course," muttered John.

"I thought we'd heard the last of them," said Lord Burghley. "Why are you still taking an interest?"

"I wanted to quest further into this matter," Philip replied. "Did you keep that sketch that Don Gustavo drew for us?"

"I keep all documents, Philip. Sometimes they are useful as evidence."

"Good. Come upstairs and let me show you what I have found to match it. I will start with a painting Her Majesty has lent me. It normally hangs in Hampton Court. It is of Queen Juana of Spain."

Burghley followed Philip into the upstairs room. There were a number of paintings in the room. He found Gustavo's sketch in his writing box and compared it to the painting of Queen Juana. Queen Juana was in a widow's dress and veil, but beneath it she had thick blonde curly hair that was severely tied back and a slightly wild look about her blue-green eyes that could not be completely erased by the artist's skill. In Gustavo's sketch the hair was loose, spilling out from under a felt cap. But the resemblance was clear enough.

"It certainly looks like her," Burghley agreed.

"Well, look at this, then." Philip led him over to the larger picture. "This is Columbus returning to the Court of King Ferdinand." Ferdinand

and Isabella were standing before his throne, with travellers on the steps below them. They were being introduced to a brown man with a feather, but no cap to put it in. The brown man was half naked and carrying a stone-tipped spear. Beside him, introducing him, were several men with travel-stained clothes, men who had recently returned from the sea.

Burghley studied the Queen carefully, but she had straight black hair and dark eyes. "That is not her," said Burghley.

"Look here," said Philip. At the other end of the canvas, near where the door was open and the three ships were at anchor in the distance, a woman lingered at the threshold. She was looking out to sea, but her head was in profile. She was dressed as one of the Queen's ladies-in-waiting, although her clothes were in brighter colours than most of them. Her nose was slightly flattened, her cheekbones strong, and her woolly blonde hair was tied back behind her. She was not looking at the strange man from the New World, or even at her own mistress, but instead she was looking out across the ocean. She didn't care what Columbus had brought back. The thing she cared about was still over the sea.

"It's her," agreed Burghley.

"The events painted here happened over seventy years ago," said Philip.

"I see the problem. So perhaps Don Gustavo's wild story is in fact true?"

"May I speak?" asked Madimi.

They both turned around. "God's wounds!" exclaimed Philip.

"You shouldn't sneak into the room like that, girl!" warned Burghley.

"I didn't sneak, sir," replied Madimi. "I was always here."

"Perhaps," conceded Burghley, "But it is hard not to form the impression that you would make a good spy."

"I *would* make a good spy," Madimi agreed. "Would you care to employ a spy?"

"What is it you want to say?"

"Lord William," said Madimi, "You are a learned man. You perhaps remember the writings of Eratosthenes, who calculated that the world was round by looking down the wells in Alexandria and Syene?"

"I am not familiar with that work," replied Burghley.

"Well, it is in Doctor Dee's library. By measuring the the height of the mid-day Sun at Alexandra and Syene, he was able to calculate what part of the Earth's circle was represented by the distance between them, and so the circumference of the world. Given the journey of Marco Polo the Spanish knew the distance from Madrid to Cathay."

"So?"

But Philip smiled. Madimi smiled back. "The Earth is twenty-five thousand miles around. So, Lord William, if it is twelve thousand miles to Cathay from Madrid via the Silk Road, then it must be thirteen thousand miles from Madrid to Cathay if you sail West."

"I see."

"So if the learned men of Ferdinand's Court knew that, why did they send Columbus with so little food and water? They must have known that he would die of thirst before he had travelled a quarter of his journey."

"I don't know," replied Burghley, disinterestedly. "Why do you think they sent him?"

Madimi pointed at the lady-in-waiting who was looking out of the door. "Because she told them to," she replied.

"She knew!" exclaimed Philip.

"She knew," agreed Madimi. "She knew there was a New World to discover. And she is looking for something."

"Then we need to make sure she doesn't get it," replied Philip. He looked over at Burghley. "Isn't that right, my lord?"

"I suppose it is. I will talk to Edward Horsey. He has a barque he is planning to send to the New World. He is a good man and he can be trusted." Burghley turned to Madimi. "And you, little mistress, please go to the good Doctor and invite him to visit us here. Tell him to bring his Spanish friend and the retainer that claims to be able to see angels." He took off a ring. "Show this ring to Doctor Dee and tell him it is mine. Tell him to come straight away, if he wishes us to believe that he is an honest man who wants to serve England and his Queen."

Madimi took the ring.

"And hurry," Burghley added. "And be sure nobody else touches my ring and that Dee does not leave your sight until he stands before us."

"Yes, lord," Madimi answered. Before either of them could react she opened the casement window and jumped out. Philip hurried over and looked down, half expecting to see her broken on the flags beneath. But she was gone.

Behind him Philip heard Burghley laughing softly to himself.

"Why did you give her your ring, my lord?"

"Because it means we know where she is. She is carrying the ring to Mortlake as we speak. Even if she can fly like a bird it will still be an hour before she returns with him. She may fly but he must walk."

"What is she?"

"She is no angel. Angels are beings of goodness and she is full of mischief. I do not know if she is an imp or some kind of airy spirit, but I think she is actually some kind of strange species of human."

"Can she be trusted?"

"She can be trusted to be true to her nature and to take care of her own interests, I am sure."

"The same could be said of anyone."

"Exactly so, young Philip. Dee told us that her kind was being persecuted by the Inquisition. Remember that old King Henry was opposed to the Lutherians? The Pope named him 'Defender of the Faith' for his opposition to them. But then things changed. Adversity makes strange bedfellows, Philip. It appears that this woman is ruling Spain, as their king-maker, and so she is our enemy. That means that Gustavo and that little angel are our allies."

"That makes sense."

"That means they are allies, Philip. That doesn't mean they are friends and most especially it does not mean they can be trusted to believe as we do."

"So what do we do?"

"They say she seeks something from the New World. If she wants it then we want it. You said you wanted to go to the New World. I think now is the time."

Philip smiled as he resisted the urge to dance. "I have dreamed of journeying to the New World, my lord."

"The only problem is that it will have to be secret. Can you go and see all those things and never speak or write of it to anyone?"

Philip took a deep breath. "For my Queen, I can."

"Good. Your father was talking of sending you to Europe. Francis Walsingham is in Paris negotiating with the House of Valois. You will write letters to your father telling how much you are learning in Paris. We will send them to Walsingham among the diplomatic papers and he will send them back at intervals. When you return you will go directly to Paris to join him there and continue your tour."

"What if he has to return?"

"Then you will have to go on to Florence or Munich, or one of the other cities a young man might take in when touring. We will have to smuggle you out of the country so you can return."

"I will do it."

"Good. Edward Horsey is a good friend and a man who can be trusted. He keeps a barque which he is re-fitting in Southampton. I will send word to him to take you and this Don Gustavo to the New World. If you can find her golden treasure and bring it back to England, then we can give her nose a tweak she will not forget."

"Could it be dangerous?"

"Hardly. England is on an island and the ships the Hawkins brothers build are the finest in Christendom. What are they going to do? Spain has strong armies, it is true, but they could hardly expect to stage an invasion of England by sea. No fleet of ships ever assembled could carry so many men."

John shook the cup and spilled the dice on the board. "A seven!" he growled. "Again!" He looked up at Christopher's smile. "How do you do it?" he demanded.

"Some numbers come up more often than others," Christopher replied.

"Are you saying that my dice are crooked?" John demanded.

"Of course not. But how many ways are there to make a twelve?"

"Only one. Two sixes."

"But how many ways are there to make a seven?"

"Four and three?"

"And three and four, and–"

"Three and four is the same as four and three, Master Stoke."

"*Doctor* Stoke, if you please. But it is not. If this one rolls a three and that one a four, that is not the same as that one rolling a three and this one rolling a four. It is twice as likely as both rolling six. And there is a two and a five and a five and a two, and a six and one and a one and six. There are six times as many ways to roll a seven as to roll a twelve. That is why a wise man bets on sevens against twelves."

"So it is not luck at all?"

"No, it is mathematics. If you play when you do not understand the mathematics of dice, then people that do understand will take your money."

"Then teach me the mathematics of dice, Doctor."

"I would prefer that you learn to find better ways of accumulating money. The man who goes on a voyage knowing the mathematics of dice may win many games against his crew-mates as he returns from Hispaniola, but if he is too good at winning what chance that he will ever see the waterfront at Southampton?" Christopher watched John's face a moment to be sure he had understood. "Better is to keep the gold that is your alloted share. After all, you told me that the master's share of one good voyage of a boat like the *Dragonfly* should make the fortune of a man. If you were careful with your gold you would never need to work again."

They both looked up as the door opened and Edward pulled aside the curtain. He looked at the dice on the tabletop. "Doctor Stoke, I would have thought better of you."

"You see dice, Master Horsey, but you don't see any coins. We are discussing the science of fortune."

"I... see. Well, now you can discuss the science of navigation. Prepare this boat to sail. And tell me where I can find Captain Ranse."

John stood up, eagerly. "We can be ready to sail with the tide tomorrow morning," he replied. "Where are we going? Hispaniola? San Juan de Ulúa?"

"Mortlake," Edward replied. He turned and left.

"Where is Mortlake?" asked Christopher.

"On the Thames," said John.

They landed between Westminster and the Embankment. They secured the ropes and the men lent their shoulders to the capstan, dragging the boat well up in the river's ooze. When they were close enough they put down a gangplank so that Master Horsey could walk ashore without getting his breeches muddy.

A kindly-looking old gentleman was waiting for them and took Horsey and Ranse away. He had three younger companions: a rather scruffy man with a thick country accent, an intense dark fellow who seemed incapable of smiling, and a handsome man with fair hair who was rather too well dressed for a voyage at sea. John did not take too much notice of them: Ranse would tell him what he needed to know. But first he set off to find himself water. The barrels should be topped off before they departed.

By the time the water and fresh provisions were loaded the *Dragonfly* had started to list as her keel settled on the river bottom. The tide was going out. Christopher spoke to John.

"When is the earliest we will be able to sail?" he asked.

"The tide turned only a couple of hours ago," John replied. "The *Dragonfly* will not be able to be floated again until dawn."

"Then the captain will have no objection to my sleeping one last night in a proper bed."

"I don't know how you are going to survive months at sea, Master Stoke."

"*Doctor* Stoke, if you please. I will survive all right. I have endured worse. But being able to endure is no reason to seek discomfort when there is no need. I want to sleep in a proper bed."

"Suit yourself. It's your money. But if you come aboard with a dose of the pox, you will have to doctor yourself."

Christopher shuddered. "That is not what I wanted at all."

"Good, because the waterside taverns of London are as rife with pox as Amsterdam or Genoa. Do not be tempted. Your one night of passion will lead to bitterness and regret."

Christopher shuddered again. "Have no fear of that."

John looked at him more carefully. "Well, try not to get robbed either." he added. "I will send someone for you if you don't return with the tide."

"Thank you," Christopher replied. He turned to go towards the nearest inn just as Ranse came out. He looked at Christopher with an expression of disappointment. "Where are you going?" he demanded.

"I want to spend one last night in a proper bed."

"With a proper companion, I suppose."

"Nothing of the sort," Christopher objected. "I just want my comfort."

"Good. Well, see you are back by first light," Ranse warned. "We sail with the morning tide. It's going to be a long voyage: Hispaniola and back."

"I will be there," Christopher promised.

"See that you are." Ranse seemed to remember his companions. "These are our passengers." He indicated the fair haired young man. "This is Philip Sidney," he said.

"The poet?" asked Christopher.

"I have scribbled a few lines," Philip replied, with surprise in his voice. "None of my words have been shared with the world."

Christopher put his hand to his mouth and John watched as his ears and cheeks became pink. Ranse grunted and indicated the dark companion. "This is Gustavo de Flores. Master Horsey believes he can act as something of a native guide."

"Good evening," said Gustavo, in accented English.

"Good evening," replied Christopher.

"And this," continued Ranse, "is Barnabas Saul, an apprentice of Doctor Dee, the mathematician and navigator. I am not quite sure why Master Horsey thinks we need a navigator on board, but if I catch him keeping a chart I will have him thrown overboard." He turned to the scruffy young man. "You understand that, young man?"

"I would not dream of it, Captain," Saul replied.

"See that you don't." Ranse turned back towards the *Dragonfly* and walked away. He looked back from the gangplank. "First light," he reminded them. "If you are not there I will go without you."

"First light," smiled Saul. "Perhaps there is time for a small beer," he suggested.

They followed him into the nearest inn.

$$- 4 -$$

To Sail Atlantis

Jane Fisher's Diary,
London,
Monday 19 May 1572 (Julian Calendar).

So in a few hours we sail for Hispaniola. Nobody has seen through my disguise as yet. I am well disguised – I am sure that nobody could spot that I am a girl dressed as a man. When I first agreed to this voyage the idea made me laugh. It is, after all, the biggest maritime cliché that a girl who fancies herself a pirate could live out. Looking at the size of the boat that I must share with fifty companions, all of them male, I wonder if even my disguise will last.

After our disappointment at being ordered to Mortlake we collected three men, special passengers to take to the New World, in search of some golden prize: el Dorado. *How can I describe my companions? Gustavo is dark and handsome, but tortured by the memory of his lost love. In his sleep he cries out to her in Spanish, telling her that he loves her and promising that he will kill her. But of course he has no name for his lover's killer other than the name she has stolen. No wonder his grief is so lost and confused.*

If Gustavo is tortured by the dark side of love, Barnabas is tortured by the dark side of everything. I understand that he is a lost soul, confused by the cruel morality of his own fragmented culture, but he has embraced it. The darkness in his heart is like a contagion, like a spiritual taint that I feel could rub off on any of us. He will not be an easy companion for fifty men confined in a wooden box no bigger than a modest apartment. I fear someone will put a knife in his neck one night and, when he makes my skin crawl, I wonder if it could be me. But I pity him too.

The Captain is a dour Puritan, his quartermaster is a giant of a man whose physical presence keeps the crew in check, and the doctor is, of course, widely acknowledged to be a fool. How much he is blasted for a fool depends on the individual crewman and, it seems, his liking for cider.

Time will tell though: we are unlikely to return to England's cool greens for a year or more.

And then there is Philip. Oh God, Philip! He is my personal temptation, the worst sort of trap for someone in my position. When I first saw him I realised how dangerous he is. He is handsome, with beautiful eyes and a soft dreamy mouth, but his mind is so quick and his manners so gentle. He is an athlete, a skilled horseman and deadly with a sword or a bow. And, somehow, I have to live close to him for maybe a year, in the tropical heat, without him realising how much heat I have for our young courtier. I cannot break my disguise, not even if I wanted to, and the sort of misunderstandings it would produce – well, let us say that it would be bloody inconvenient.

We haven't even started yet and I dread how it will be when the adventure starts. I have to get to know every one of these boys and men and I also know that half of them will never return to Southampton. Who will be first? I will do my best to protect them, take care of them as if I was their own mother, but it will break my heart when we lose our first. In truth, even if he is Barnabas.

Courage, Jane. They cannot suspect. Your disguise is too good. Have courage and the mission will soon be over, and you can go home and get some serious R. and R.

"Christopher!" Philip banged on the door again. "Come on, wake up! We will need to be going soon."

"I'm awake," called Christopher. "I will be down in a couple of minutes."

When Philip reached Gustavo's door he found the Spaniard already dressed and waiting. He opened the door and came out. "Where are they?" he asked.

"Christopher is awake. I do not know about Barnabas. When I called at his door it was a woman who answered."

"Was it that one?" asked Gustavo, pointing with a nod of the head as a half-dressed girl left Barnabas' room.

"No. That is another one."

"Let us get him up, then."

Philip and Gustavo marched over to the woman before she could close the door. She cringed but they pushed past her. Barnabas was in the bed, naked. "Come on," said Gustavo. "If you miss the boat you will have to answer to your master."

"I am not afraid of my 'master'," whined Barnabas.

"If you are not afraid of Lord Burghley, you are a fool," suggested Philip.

"All right, all right," grumbled Barnabas. "But I paid for five girls and I have only had four."

Gustavo strode into the room and cuffed Barnabas around the ear. "You miserable dog," he said. "Get dressed or I'll drag you to the boat like that."

They met Christopher in the hall, carrying his bag. The four of them went out into the cool twilight. When they had gone to bed the *Dragonfly* had stood at a rakish angle but in the growing light they could see that her masts stood upright again. The gangplank was gently rocking and swaying as the incoming tide swirled around her hull. Men in boats stood ready to drag them off the mud and into the centre of the Thames.

They found their cabins and then, with a shout, the ropes on shore were loosed and the men out in the river began to row. The cables tightened with each stroke. Just as Philip was wondering if they would ever come loose they all felt a shudder as they slipped down into the water. The men out in the boats continued to row.

Ranse spoke to John. "Get the men ready with the bow anchor," he called. "I want us underway as soon as the tide turns."

John shouted at the sleepy men and they dragged the heavy anchor onto the foc'sle deck. With a splash it fell into the Thames and the cable took up the slack. The *Dragonfly* slowly turned to face downstream. "You there, Mark Tanner," Ranse called, "Watch that anchor rope. When it slackens, call out."

"Aye, Captain," the young man called back.

"Keep men by the capstan. And as soon as the tide turns I want the foresail," Ranse told John.

John ordered men into the rigging. They waved at the tug-men as they rowed back to the shore to fetch the next boat. Then they stood quietly, shivering in the cold damp air, until Mark the Tanner's Son called out in a clear voice. "It's slack, Captain."

"Get that sail out!" Ranse called. "And get the anchor up." Christopher watched as the cloth fell from the spar and experienced hands caught the sheets and secured them. Men lent their shoulders to the capstan and the anchor came free of the Thames. The morning breeze filled the sail and the boat creaked. They hardly felt the motion but behind them a wake appeared. Then slowly, slowly, London began to slip past.

They were on their way.

* * *

They had been at sea for three weeks and the companions had fallen into a routine. Gustavo found his favourite spot at the stern rail, looking out at the wake of the boat and, beyond it, the horizon that hid his beloved Spain and the unmarked grave of his girl. Behind him the Sun was setting and the sky ahead darkened. The first stars would soon be visible. He could hear the shouts of the men, growing louder and more incoherent as the evening's rum ration took its toll. From the bows, below decks, Christopher Stoke's voice rose and began to sing

> *A captain bold in Halifax,*
> *Who dwelt in country quarters,*
> *Seduced a maid who hanged herself,*
> *One morning in her garters.*
> *His wicked conscience smoted him,*
> *He lost his stomach daily.*
> *He took to drinking turpentine,*
> *And thought upon Miss Bailey.*

It was a rather disreputable, bawdy song, and Gustavo knew that the puritan Captain Ranse would not approve. But he could hear John Overy and the men laughing and joining in. He saw a shadow and looked up. Philip was there. Gustavo made room and Philip sat beside him.

> *One night, betimes he went to bed,*
> *For he had caught a fever,*
> *Said he, "I am a handsome man,*
> *"And I'm a gay deceiver."*
> *His candle just at twelve o'clock,*
> *Began to burn quite palely,*
> *A ghost stepped up beside his bed,*
> *And said, "Behold! Miss Bailey!"*

"Do you think she has any kind of conscience?" Gustavo asked.
"Who?"
"The witch who murdered my beloved."
"I don't know," Philip replied. "Many believe that as a man grows old his conscience becomes dulled. How old is she?"
"More than six thousand years, she said."

"I think the lady exaggerates. It has been known since the days of the Venerable Bede that the Earth cannot be more than four thousand years older than Christ. So, even if she was in the garden with Adam and Eve she couldn't be more than five thousand five hundred and seventy-two."

"Madimi said that she heard about the witch from her grandmother, who had heard from her grandmother and so on back for generations. Even if she exaggerated her age she still must be hundreds of years old."

"And her conscience has completely degenerated."

"She had come to kill me because I knew too much. But she pretended to be my Eva. She played with me like a cat plays with a mouse." Gustavo turned around and scowled. "Why did she have to do that?"

> *"Avaunt, Miss Bailey!" then he cried.*
> *"You cannot fright me really!"*
> *"Dear Captain Smith," the ghost replied*
> *"You've used me most ungenteely.*
> *"The coroner's quest was hard on me,*
> *"Because I acted frailly,*
> *"And Parson Briggs won't bury me,*
> *"'Though I'm a dead Miss Bailey."*

"What did you do with her body?" Gustavo whispered to the ocean and the wind.

"She is at peace, I am sure."

"How could her soul be at peace? Why would that mad witch bother with a Christian burial? Surely someone who ordered that little Madimi and her children be left unbaptised would have no remorse about my beloved Eva's rest."

> *"Mistress," said he, "Since you and I,*
> *"Our accounts now must close,*
> *"I have a shiny sovereign in,*
> *"My regimental clothes.*
> *"Twill bribe the sexton for your grave."*
> *The ghost then vanished gaily,*
> *Saying "Bless you, wicked Captain Smith,*
> *"Remember poor Miss Bailey. "*

Philip made no reply. But Gustavo whispered, "*Est et alia vanitas quae fit super terram sunt iusti quibus multa proveniunt quasi opera egerint imporium et sunt impii qui ita securi sunt quasi iustorium facta habeant sed et hoc vanissimum iudicio.*"

"For God shall judge all works and secret things, whether they be good or evil," Philip translated. He looked at Gustavo, mug in hand. "They say Solomon was the wisest of kings."

"It's true, Philip", Gustavo replied. "The righteous get what the wicked deserve and the wicked get what the righteous deserve."

"For now, my friend. But both Daniel and John tell us that man will not live the same forever. God will judge us all. The church of Rome has grown fat and wicked – pardon me, but you know it is true – so God has chosen England, Holland, and other places to overturn them. Babylon trembles and will surely fall. Then God will pour his wrath upon her."

"But what about us? How do we bear these injustices?"

"God gives us strength to bear what we cannot change."

"It seems that God has ordained love, but love goes to mischance and is lost as often as it is found. My love lies in the grave and I do not even know where that grave is."

"No, Gustavo," Philip replied. "Your love awaits you in heaven. But first you need to win her, by doing the work that God has set you."

"Do you really believe that?" Gustavo asked.

"Yes, I do. Think about King Solomon, Gustavo. Remember God when you are young was the advice that this most wise of monarchs offered. Our time comes, the earth returns to earth and the soul returns to God. That is where we will all go. Most of us wonder if we will have friendship waiting for us there, but you know that you have." Gustavo could see that he believed it and, listening to him, Gustavo believed it too, for a moment at least.

"She waits for you, Gustavo. All you have to do is win your place beside her."

He hoped it would not be too long.

The midday Sun beat down on the bleached timbers of the *Dragonfly* and glittered on the blue water that stretched from the waves around their hull to the edge of the sky. Ranse stood on the deck and reckoned the height of the Sun above the horizon. He smiled a rueful smile. "Make a course a little to the South of East, John," he told his quartermaster. "And keep a lookout. We will see land in the next day or two."

Even to turn a little South of East meant re-setting the sails as well as the wheel, and John's bellow sent two dozen men up the rigging. Ranse watched patiently as they worked then, as they came down again, he looked down at the lodestone. "When everything is set, perhaps you and the other gentlemen will join me in my cabin."

"Certainly," replied John. "Captain, does your definition of 'gentleman' include Master Saul?"

"I'm afraid it does, John. It also includes that Spanish fellow."

"I see."

Once the sails were set, the lookout posted and a trusted pair of hands on the wheel, John came into the Captain's cabin. Gustavo and Christopher, Philip and Barnabas followed. Somehow they all squeezed around the map table. Ranse had put away his chart and his log: all that was on the table was a printed Bible. Ranse looked down at it and began to read out loud.

"There were tyrants in the world in those days. For after that the children of God had gone in unto the daughters of men and had begotten them children. The same children were the mightiest of the world and men of renown. And when the Lord saw that the wickedness of man was increased upon the earth and that all the imagination and thoughts of his heart was only evil continually, he repented that he had made man upon the earth and sorrowed in his heart.

"And said: I will destroy mankind which I have made from of the face of the earth: both man, beast, worm and fowl of the air, for it repenteth me that I have made them."

"The story of Noah," said Christopher. "But you hope to make land, Captain."

"I have been told a very strange story," said Ranse. "I was forbidden from discussing it when I was still in England. But now I must know. Where are we going and what will we do when we get there?"

"Noe is the right story," said Gustavo. "For our enemy is the last survivor from that flood. It may be true that she is the mightiest in the world. She is as strong as any knight, but she is also a witch. She told me that she was six thousand years old. She is the last survivor of Atlantis."

"Noah's Flood covered the whole world," objected Philip. "How could she have survived that?"

"I do not know. She is a witch."

"I have never seen any reason to be afraid of witches," Ranse replied. "I was told there was treasure. But I was also told that this is something to do with those long lost days."

"It is." agreed Saul, suddenly. They turned to look at him. "What we are looking for is the Pyramids of Atlantis," he said. "Captain Ranse, you know this land. Find me pyramids and I will find your treasure."

"There are no pyramids this side of Hispaniola," said Ranse. "The only place I have seen a pyramid is in San Juan de Ulúa. And there is no welcome for an English boat there."

"Why not?" asked Christopher.

"Four years ago we sailed there," Ranse explained. "We were a trading expedition financed partly by men of the City of London, and partly by Her Majesty. We were four ships: I commanded the *William and John* for Hawkins. Rob Barrett commanded the *Jesus of Lubeck*, one of King Harry's fleet. Hawkins took the *Minion*, another of Her Majesty's ships; and, after the death of their previous master from the poisoned dart of a savage, the *Judith* was commanded by the Drake brothers.

"We were caught in a storm that lasted four days, on the leg from Cartagena to San Juan de Ulúa. The storms in these lattitudes are something that nobody who has sailed the calm waters of home would believe, the winds are so fierce. The wind did as it pleased with us for a day and, when it calmed, we were alone. We were sure the others had foundered: we counted ourselves lucky to have survived. So we repaired the ship as best we could and set our course for England.

"But, unknown to us, the other three had made port at San Juan de Ulúa, and been welcomed cordially by the Spanish. The governor, Martin Enriquez, greeted them with salute from the harbour guns. With the *Jesus* strained in the storm and taking in water, they were grateful to get the shelter of the port. Governor Enriquez made truce with Hawkins. They agreed to allow the English to repair their ships in exchange for not plundering the port and for the return of the Spanish hostages they had collected on the venture.

"Well, they learned the value of Enriquez' word. That is, none at all. The rest of the Spanish fleet arrived next day and the Spanish men launched an attack from the island where the ships were tied up. The *Minion* came under fire first. Hawkins' crew were quick to cut the bow ropes and warp out by the anchor ropes to get clear of the shore battery. This left the *Jesus* exposed to fire. Barratt attempted to follow Hawkins' lead. But the *Jesus of Lubeck* was an old, slow ship – as I said, one of King Harry's old fleet – and fouled from too long in this Southern water as well as strained from the storm. They could not move her quickly enough. The Spanish guns tore her rigging to pieces and the crew took to the pinnaces.

"The other two ships managed to escape, although both were heavily overloaded with men from the *Jesus*. The Drakes took the *Judith* away and the *Minion* needed to put men ashore before they could return home. Many of these men were captured by the Spanish and ill-used. And all the sailors of England remember the perfidity of the Spanish governor."

Gustavo sat with a tight expression on his face and his hands balled in fists. Christopher was wondering what he could say to break the mood when Saul recited: -

"Two kings are locked in dire conflict"
"North and South, to share a land"
"Such bitter war, such mighty weapons"
"Now pyramids in darkness stand"

The rest of them frowned, although Philip seemed to smile too. "What does it mean?" asked Christopher.

"It means we can either look North or look South. If Captain Ranse does not wish to go North and meet perfidious Spanish governors, we should look for pyramids in the South. If we do not find what we seek, then we can return to pyramids in the North."

"Land ho!" the lookout cried.

Ranse came hurrying forward, his spy-glass in his hand. He extended it and looked ahead. "Get the lead line," he said. "And John, get those top-sails furled, too. I don't want us stuck on some reef."

"Aye, captain," replied Overy. He shouted up the orders to the crew and the top-sails were taken in and secured to the yards. The wake behind the *Dragonfly* settled down. A man stood at the bow with a line and a weight. He rubbed a bit of tallow into a hole at the bottom of the weight and threw it overboard. He counted the knots in the rope as he let it down, until there was no more left. "Twenty fathoms clear," he called.

Ranse was at the wheel, looking out at the waves and trying to spot reefs by the shapes of the surf above them. The land ahead was flat but with a rock to the north. Ranse steered to the north of the rock and listened to the linesman. "By the deep nineteen fathoms," called the linesman. "White sand," he added when he had the weight in his hand. He cast again. "By the mark seventeen fathoms," he called.

The little island came up on their port side. It could not have been more than half a mile wide. Ranse steered them past the big rock and they saw a beach with a stream running down it. "By the deep six fathoms," the linesman called. "White sand."

The beach was in front of them. "Get ready to turn to port," Ranse called to John.

As the men re-set the sails Ranse turned the wheel hard down. The boat turned, the sails flapped a little and they were heading towards the beach. "Get the anchor ready at the bow," he called.

"By the mark eight fathoms. White sand." The beach got closer and, ahead, they could hear the surf. "By the mark six fathoms," the linesman called.

"Get the sails in," Ranse called. "Drop the anchor."

The anchor plunged into the water and they drew the line with the capstan. The sails were furled and the boat slowly turned back into the wind, the anchor rope taut. "Get the boat un-stowed," Ranse said. "We need to get water and I am sure the men will want to stretch their legs."

"Aye, sir," said John, happily.

"Now pull!" shouted John. The men hauled on their oars and the dinghy leaped over the wave. As they came down the other side John jumped down into water up to his waist and hauled the painter. The other men secured their oars and dragged the boat up the sand. "Robin, help me with this barrel. The rest of you, go and get lost. But try not to get killed. I will fire one of my pistols when we are ready to go. Laggards will be marooned. Now go!"

With whoops the men ran away across the sand and into the trees. "Why do I get to drag barrels?" he grumbled.

"Because of the size of you. And because you are a troublemaker. I've seen the way you have been looking at Jim and Mark."

"They are like a couple of women. And you know what they will be doing as soon as they can find a quiet spot."

"That is no concern of ours."

"It's not natural. We should catch them and–"

"We should live and let live, Robin Smith."

The barrel was on a frame and they picked it up by the staves that stuck out front and back. John stood at the back and Robin led. They found their way to the stream but there was nowhere they could get the barrel under a cataract. They had to use the buckets and bail water into the barrel.

But Robin carried on grumbling. "By now Jim will have stuck his–"

"Are you jealous?" asked John.

Robin leaped to his feet with a roar of rage. John stood more calmly but no slower. They stood either side of the barrel. "I should–"

"If you think you can," replied John. He had his hand on his pistol.

The two men stared into each other's faces a moment. Then Robin looked down.

"Now let's get this barrel filled," John said.

The old man led the younger one through the trees. They found a hollow where a large tree had fallen, leaving a hole in the canopy above them that allowed through a patch of brightness in a world of shadow. The older man sat down slowly while his young companion bounded around him like an excited puppy.

"Sit down, young Mark," the old man said. "Let us see what we have to share."

"I can't help it," the younger man replied. "It has been so long since I have stood on dry land."

"Well, come here and sit on dry land, my boy. Have something to eat and drink."

The younger man sat down. "And what have you brought us, Mother?" he smiled.

"I packed your favourites, of course. Nice, crunchy ship's biscuit and Adam's finest ale."

"Not cider, then?" the younger man smiled.

"I have been at sea for twenty years," the old man chuckled, "but I never drank cider in the middle of a voyage."

"The doctor says it will help us to be healthy. He says it will protect us from scurvy."

"There hasn't been much scurvy on this voyage," the older man replied. "But some voyages are worse than others. It might be a coincidence."

"I don't want to think about voyages," the younger man answered. "I want to sit with you and imagine we are back in England."

"Of course you do, beloved."

When Mark's tears broke, Jim was ready. He had seen loneliness in young lads many times before and he knew what to do. He held the young man by the shoulders as his heart cried out. "There, lad," he whispered. The sound of Mark's grief covered over the other sounds behind him.

John Overy couldn't deny Robin his time on shore just on the basis of his suspicions, but he knew things were not right. He let Robin walk until he was almost out of sight among the trees and then he followed.

Robin wasn't hard to follow. John could see that he was not wandering and enjoying the air and the land. He was searching, quartering the island, looking for something. John checked the pistols in his belt.

It didn't take Robin long to find them. He heard the boy crying out and he knew he must already be in the old man's power. He broke into a run. His knife was in his hand. He saw the back of the old man and the top of the young man's head in the old man's arms. "They have committed an abomination and shall die for it!" he roared at them, punctuating his speech with blows of the knife. "Their blood be upon their head!"

Mark danced out of the way and reached for his own knife. "Murder!" he screamed. "Murder!"

"You gave yourself to his filthy lusts, boy!" Robin roared. "You deserve to die, both of you." He lunged at the boy just as John Overy burst out of the trees behind him.

"Hey," shouted John. "Pick on someone your own size." He aimed a kick at the seat of Robin's breeches. Robin stumbled and fell on top of Mark. John reached down and grabbed Robin's hair. He pulled him to his feet and slammed him face-first into a tree. He looked around for Robin's knife, then he saw it protruding from Mark's jerkin.

Mark looked down and his hands reached up. "I'm murdered," he whimpered.

John feared it was true. But he said, "Leave it there, lad. Let the surgeon pull it out." His hands found rope and he lashed Robin's wrists together.

The other men came through the woods. "What happened?" one of them asked.

"Robin attacked them," John replied. "He's been spoiling for a fight this whole voyage."

"Robin knows right from wrong," one man muttered. "He reads his Bible."

"What is wrong with a touch of homesickness?" John demanded. "I didn't see anything more than that and I was not more than ten yards behind him."

John looked at the men's faces. He picked the ones who shared Robin's obsession with imagined sin to man the oars but he chose two more sympathetic souls to carry the poor lad. By the time they arrived at the *Dragonfly* the boy had blood in his mouth. John carried him into the surgeon's cabin.

Christopher was writing. He looked up and he gathered everything off the table. "Put him here," he said. "Bring me boiling water, pitch, canvas and thread, a hot iron and a half-ration of rum." He looked down at the boy. "Now lie still and we'll get this mess cleaned up," he said.

"Am I going to die?" Mark whispered.

"We're all going to die," Christopher Stoke replied. "But I would think you will live to see England's shores."

"Do you promise?"

"I promise, Mark Tanner."

By the time John returned with the things the surgeon had asked for the boy was lying motionless, staring at the ceiling. "Can he hear us?" John asked.

"He can, but he won't remember," replied Christopher. "His eyes are open but he is dreaming and can feel no pain."

"A herb?"

"Something like that."

With expert hands Christopher cut the jerkin off the boy to uncover the skin. The knife had gone in at an angle and he hoped it would not be too deep. He prepared dressings and put his own knife into the spirit that John had brought.

"Will he live?" John asked, unbelieving.

"I hope so," Christopher replied, as he tied a scarf around his face and soaked his hands in rum. "If no major blood vessel is involved I should be able to stop the bleeding. I think his lung may partially have collapsed. I can't use suction so I will have to improvise an appropriate dressing that will release the trapped air. He is young and will heal well in time, if we can avoid infection. I will do my best."

John watched as the surgeon worked. He expected Christopher to sew the wound but he didn't. Instead he touched it with the hot iron here and there to stop the bleeding, then covered it with oilcloth soaked in rum, which he sealed down on three sides with hot pitch. Finally he turned to the boy. "Listen to my voice, Mark Tanner," he said. "I will count down from ten and, as you hear my voice, you will fall into a deep sleep. You will sleep until morning and will wake with no fear. Ten, nine, eight, seven, six..."

As the surgeon counted Mark closed his eyes and began to snore gently. The dressing flapped a little with a sound of air bubbling out. But as he breathed in again the dressing held.

"Help me get him off the table," said Christopher. "I want him to sleep in my cot. He will need total bed rest tonight. Then we can sew the wound and he can get up."

"Where will you sleep? You can't sleep among the men or it will be your own ribs you are removing knives from."

"Do they hate the taste of cider so much?"

John sighed. "Some men's lust is directed not at women but at boys. I don't care myself but, in the close quarters of a boat, some men care very much."

"I am not what you think I am," replied Christopher.

"I don't care what you are, doctor," replied John. "But some of the men care very much. So you must be careful."

From the island they steered south until they encountered the main. Then they followed the coast along for two weeks. They only had two encounters on the way: a Spanish caravel that they quickly captured and a little open boat that surrendered immediately they were threatened. The merchant spat and called Gustavo a traitor until Ranse ordered him locked away below decks on his own boat.

Ranse spent the last day fretting on the quarterdeck, worrying with his spy-glass.

"What are you looking for?" Christopher asked.

"Somewhere to put in and re-provision, doctor," Ranse replied.

"Are you looking for a particular place?"

"Yes, I am. I heard tell from some men that there is a secret harbour that is safe from all winds, known only to the English. It will be a good place to re-provision – if it has not been betrayed!"

The ship's bell had rung three times before Ranse spotted what he was looking for. "Turn south," he ordered. The men hurried to turn the boat around, almost doubling back on themselves around a headland. Christopher and Gustavo watched as they entered the mouth of a river. "Get the linesman to the prow!"

The linesman began to call the soundings. When they were in the middle of the channel Ranse ordered them to turn south-east, and they followed the channel as it narrowed. They passed an island on the starboard side with little room to turn. Then on their port side a bay opened up, perfectly concealed from a view from the sea.

And, perfectly concealed in it, were two boats. They saw men hurrying to warp the boats out, shake out the sails and run out the cannon.

Ranse gave the orders and the *Dragonfly*'s own cannon were prepared. With no room to turn around, there was nothing else for it but to fight.

— 5 —

The Secret Harbour

The *Dragonfly* had the gun-ports open and only a little sail, just enough to be able to turn. The other two boats were a barque rather smaller than the *Dragonfly* and a smaller boat. They heard the master of the other ship shout orders.

"Get those cannon out, if you don't want to rot in a Spanish prison!" he screamed in an accent thick with the West Country.

"Hey!" called out Ranse. "Who are you calling 'Spanish'?"

"Who is there?" the other shouted back.

"I am Captain Ranse, an honest Englishman and Protestant like yourselves. This is Edward Horsey's boat."

"Stand down, lads!" whooped the other master. "Well met, Captain Ranse! I am Captain Drake and this is the *Pascha*, out of Plymouth. Welcome to our Port Pheasant. Come aboard when you have made yourselves secure."

Once the *Dragonfly* was secure beside the *Swan* and the *Pascha*, they went ashore. A rough-built pentagonal fort had been constructed from logs, with one side open to the sea. They rowed towards this and they were welcomed inside. Both captains were called Drake, brothers Francis and John. A table had been set out for them, with plate and cloth and musicians to play on the viol whilst they ate.

"Before we begin," Ranse explained, "You must understand that our voyage here is a secret of the State. The details of my passengers and my destination must not be shared, by the command of Her Majesty."

"I accept that," Francis replied. John nodded his agreement.

"Good. These companions are John Overy, master of my ship; Barnabas Saul, an assistant of the navigator Doctor Dee; my own surgeon, Doctor Stoke; and this is Don Gustavo Diego de Flores."

"*El Draque,*" Gustavo said.

The younger Drake looked shocked. "You are Spanish?" he asked.

"I am," Gustavo replied. "But I am not going to betray you to Spain. I believe Spain has been deceived by an enemy that lives among them. In loyalty to Spain I oppose Spain."

"Spain and England are almost at war," the older Drake cautioned.

"That is a war that should not be fought," Gustavo replied. "And the Moors in Spain have a saying. It says 'The enemy of my enemy is my friend.' I have agreed to help England to defeat the purpose of Spain's enemy."

"Tell me about this enemy," Drake replied.

"I discovered that the Atlanteans still walk the Earth. My enemy – Spain's enemy – is an Atlantean witch who has ruled the Catholic Church for many centuries."

"Some mad old woman is running the Roman church?"

"Captain Drake, you are thinking of poor peasant women who are picked out by the Inquisition. This woman appears young and beautiful, but she has the experience of centuries. I do not know if she rules the whole of the Church but I am sure she is behind the Inquisition. She certainly is the power behind the Spanish throne and has been since the days of Ferdinand. She is behind the discovery of the New World and she has no wish to share the treasures of the New World with the English."

"I am not afraid of any witches," Francis Drake replied. "No enchantments can withstand the combination of strong faith and strong arms." He looked around his men. "And we have plenty of both."

"I hope you are never proved wrong," Gustavo replied.

"Captain Drake," Philip interrupted, "You can see that our friend Gustavo is loyal, even if you feel your faith will protect you. As I said, some of the details of our voyage are affairs of state."

"Well," Drake replied, "I wonder if these 'affairs of state' would prevent you from sharing those treasures of the New World. We have in mind a little adventure and 'the harvest is great but the labourers are few'."

"I see," said Philip. "What sort of adventure do you have planned?"

"The mountains of the New World are filled with gold and silver," Drake replied. "The Spanish tax the people of these lands for their gold and silver and it is gathered in two great treasure-houses. One at San Juan de Ulúa, five hundred leagues from here. The other is at Nombre de Dios, less than a week West of this fine harbour.

"Every year, in the late summer, the Spanish send a fleet to the New World to collect this bounty. They are due to arrive in the next few weeks.

Of course the time it takes them to cross the ocean depends on the weather but they have never arrived before the end of July."

"The winds this year have been extraordinarily favourable," Ranse countered.

"They have," agreed Drake. "But we are only at the end of the second week in July. Our ships are designed by the Hawkins brothers and are much more able to use the wind. Unless the wind was exactly perfect for them they could not arrive before the 25th of July. The gold is in the treasure-house in Nombre de Dios, waiting to be collected."

"So what is your plan, then?" asked Ranse. "Wait for the fleet to return and cut out some strays?"

"Not at all," Drake replied. "I instructed craftsmen to construct three boats for me, but to cut the timbers without assembling them. Now my carpenter is assembling them here. They will be small and shallow enough in draught to sail right up to the beaches in Nombre de Dios. We will come ashore, break into the treasure house, and fill our boats. Perhaps, with your shallop to add to our three pinnaces, we might take it all."

"Well," said Philip, glancing over at Ranse, "That is certainly an audacious plan."

"Audacious is one word," agreed Ranse. "There are others."

"Captain Ranse," Drake smiled, "We have no risk for our own vessels. You captured the shallop on the way to this harbour, I don't doubt. It has a Spanish look about it. We will take our ships to a nearby island and put such crew as wish to volunteer aboard the pinnaces and your shallop. It is they that will take the risks."

Gustavo winced a little inside as he heard Drake speak. "Perhaps Captain Ranse is concerned about the unknown situation in Nombre de Dios. It would be good strategy to take a few men into the town and see what can be discovered."

"But against that is the danger that the men will be discovered by the Spanish," Drake answered. "The Spanish do not treat their prisoners well."

"Captain Drake," Gustavo replied, "I think I can enter a town in the New World and pass myself as a Spaniard. I actually speak Spanish very well." He waited a moment for the laughter to die down. "Philip here has good Spanish too, and Christopher's Spanish is excellent. I think that we could take Captain Ranse's shallop into Nombre de Dios and find out the situation without being caught as English spies."

"All right, Mr. Gustavo, you have made your point," Drake agreed.

"He may have made his point to you," Ranse growled, "But I was given instructions by my master. Would you mind if we discuss this first?"

"Of course."

After the meal Ranse led them along the beach to a place where they could talk alone. He looked at Philip, Gustavo and Barnabas. "The Drake Brothers are not proposing to cut out a galleon that has strayed from the fleet. They are proposing to take a whole town as large as Portsmouth." Ranse looked at them carefully, watching each face in turn. "Is this a distraction from what we are here to do?" he asked.

"If we are looking for a treasure from the New World," Philip answered, "Then this is the most likely place to find it. We should insist on choosing one item from the treasure first, even if we let the Drake brothers divide the rest as they see fit. That one item could be the thing we have come here to fetch."

"It is true," agreed Gustavo. "If they have found the thing she seeks it will be in the King's treasure house, ready to take to Spain. We will not get another opportunity to search through the King's treasure house."

Ranse looked at John. "What about the men?"

"The men are certainly willing, Captain Ranse. There will be more than enough to fill the boat. We should not take more than a dozen, though, since they will limit the amount of gold we can bring back. We can pick our best men and... I wish we still had Robin Smith. He was a good man in a fight."

"Too good," snorted Ranse. "If he had kept the fighting to the Spanish you would still have him. I don't know how you saved that lad, Doctor Stoke. I would have sworn he was murdered."

"It will be weeks more before he is ready for action," Chris replied.

Philip turned to Barnabas Saul. "We think this item may have some kind of magical property. You are our expert in such matters. What do you think?"

When Barnabas Saul spoke, it was another of his wretched verses.

> *"The duck glides out across the water,"*
> *"Too late, for all the bread is gone,"*
> *"Do not be so quick to give up,"*
> *"Next year, maybe, more is won."*

"Jolly as ever," laughed John.

"I begin to understand why the Lady Cassandra was so popular," Philip added.

"I'll have none of that nonsense in front of the crew," warned Ranse. He looked at the others. "Very well," he agreed, "You can go on this adventure of the Drakes. I can spare twelve men and the shallop. But if you are captured or killed by the Spanish I will not take responsibility for your deaths."

"Nor would I expect you to," replied Philip.

Jane Fisher's Diary,
The North Coast of Panama,
Tuesday 13 July 1572 (Julian Calendar).

We have made it to the New World. I could write a book about that journey, if I had a gift for words. We lost five. Our doctor took it hard, as if he had never lost a patient before. When young Thomas fell onto the deck he lasted until after midnight, although I knew as soon as I saw him that he was doomed. To give a young man raw opium knowing he will not survive, then hold his head as he cries for the mother he will never see again, that is a side of medicine they didn't teach our doctor in college.

So today we had supper with two pirate captains. The Drake Brothers are young men in their twenties, full of fire and fine manners. I can see how any man could follow them to the ends of the Earth. Any woman too. Needless to say young Philip gets on with them very well. They are already thick with plans together. To think, I get to meet both Francis Drake and Philip Sidney, two of Tudor England's greatest warriors.

But that cannot compensate me for the sheer brutishness of life on board a Tudor boat. And when the first breath of wonder has been exhaled from my chest, all that is left is the hollow of homesickness.

They had sailed three days when they reached the Pine Islands. The marvellous weather that had brought them over the ocean seemed to have departed, but the sky was clear and the winds fair. They came around a headland and approached the harbour where Ranse would wait with the three ships until the pinnaces returned.

They could see a beach and, anchored a short way off the shore, two frigates being loaded with planks and logs. Ranse looked at Overy. "What do you think, Captain?" Overy asked.

Ranse glanced over at the *Pascha*, and saw the men scrambling up the rigging to re-set the sails. "I think the Drake Brothers will go and fetch them," he said.

"What should we do?"

"We should wait out here. If one of the boats escapes the Drakes, we should be ready to stop it. We would not want news of our presence to get as far as Nombre de Dios. Tell the men to get into the rigging and be ready to load the cannons. Furl the sails in but be ready to let them out again."

John cupped his hands to his mouth and called the orders. His raised voice and the commotion of opening gun-ports attracted the attention of their passengers. They came up on deck just as the *Pascha* and *Swan* turned towards the shore. On the shore they could see men running back to their boats. The English boats heeled over a little as the wind crossed them but Philip knew that, with the sails full, they would be making good way.

"I hope they know that harbour," Ranse growled. "We don't want to have to tow them off some sandbar."

The crews of the two frigates surrendered when they saw the English pirates bearing down on them. When it was obvious that the frigates were under English control, Ranse ordered the gun crew to stand down and steered the *Dragonfly* into the harbour. He came in much more slowly, listening to the calls from the linesman in the bow. By the time they were on the beach Drake was speaking to the prisoners.

The prisoners had been organised into two groups: the Spanish separated from the rest. The Spanish were easy to identify by their better clothing and their weapons and armour. The rest were about half from the local natives and about half slaves brought from Africa. The Drake Brothers were trying to talk to them but having difficulty making themselves understood.

"What are you trying to tell them?" Christopher asked.

"I would like to gain their assistance," he replied. "They have no more reason to love the Spanish than we do."

"Very well," Christopher answered. "I will talk to them."

Philip and Gustavo went and spoke to the Spanish prisoners. There were three of them. Gustavo looked at them with scorn. "Are they noblemen?" Philip asked.

"In Nombre de Dios, perhaps," Gustavo replied. "Many Spanish who come to the New World have no fortune. Or they are sent here because they have disgraced themselves at home."

"Criminals?"

"Criminals or debtors. Some will have been sent by their families because they have shamed them."

"And you think these three are the same?"

"I would think so." He turned to them and switched to Spanish. "*Well, gentlemen, how did you come to be sent to the New World?*"

"*Wherever my fortune has led me, I'm not a spy for the English,*" one replied.

Gustavo put his hand on the hilt of his rapier and turned to the Englishmen. "*This man would like a sword,*" he said in Spanish.

"*I meant no offence, sir,*" the Spaniard replied.

"*Good. Perhaps you will answer our questions and keep your opinions to yourself.*"

"*Of course. I came to the New World because I did not have a big enough fortune to marry the girl I loved.*"

"*I see. And how long have you been here?*"

"*Twelve years, sir.*"

"*And is she waiting for you?*"

The other man laughed. "*She wrote to me in six months. She had found another. Women are not to be trusted.*"

"*Some women are not to be trusted, perhaps,*" Gustavo agreed. "*But it is hard to learn the whole story from a letter.*" He looked away a moment and saw Christopher talking to the slaves. They were all sat around, watching him, entranced. Gustavo turned back to the three merchants. "*Anyway, what news from Nombre de Dios?*"

"*The whole place is astir, sir,*" the man answered. "*The attacks from the* Cimmarones *are only getting worse, and some high-born guest from the court of King Philip is coming to stay with the Governor. It is as if they know: as if they are attacking more to embarrass the Governor before the King's courtier.*"

"*Perhaps they do know,*" Gustavo smiled. "*This courtier will arrive with some bodyguard?*"

"*I am sure there will be some knights, sir.*"

"*I see.*" Gustavo turned to Philip. "How much of that did you understand," he asked in English.

"Most of it, I think," Philip replied. "I understood that there is a courtier visiting with a bodyguard."

"That could make it harder to take the town," Gustavo warned. "It depends on how good the bodyguard is."

"How will we find out?"

"I think we will have to visit Nombre de Dios." He turned to the Spaniards. "*Thank you, gentlemen,*" he said.

They walked over to see how Christopher was getting on. The slaves were getting on one of the frigates. "What happened?" Philip asked.

"Your doctor has made a treaty with them," Francis Drake replied. "They have their freedom in exchange for allegiance to the crown of England."

"So where are they going?"

"They are to be put ashore. It is too far for them to walk to Nombre de Dios in time to give the alarm, but they will spread the word that the English gave them freedom."

The town of Nombre de Dios spread along the shoreline and climbed up the hill to surround a church. There were small boats coming and going and one large merchantman anchored a way offshore. John had expected that it would be hard to handle the shallop with such an inexperienced crew, but he was surprised to discover that Christopher was a very capable sailor. With Philip and Barnabas' untutored help the four of them managed the little boat handily enough.

Twenty-five leagues behind them the Drake brothers were drilling their men with the weapons and armour they had brought with them from England. They would follow along the coast in the evening and wait in the mouth of the Rio Francisco. John had agreed to get their boat back before sunset. Which meant they had a few hours to look over the town and find out if this courtier had arrived.

Gustavo sat in the bow of the boat, looking out at the town. He had his best hat on and his cloak over one shoulder.

"You might lend a hand with this sail," John suggested.

"I might but I won't," Gustavo replied. "The man I am pretending to be would not help his servants."

John grumbled but Christopher whispered some reply and John fell silent. Barnabas just smirked. John steered the boat towards the quay and Philip came forward, beside Gustavo, ready with the rope. Just as Barnabas was sure they would ram the quay, Christopher loosened the sail and John sharply turned the tiller. The little boat swung around, the sail flapped ineffectually, and they drifted sideways and bumped gently against the quay.

Gustavo climbed up. A man was coming over to see them. He seemed about to ask questions, but Gustavo spoke first. "*You, there,*" he called in Spanish, "*Are you the harbour-master?*"

Christopher could see the effect Gustavo's voice had on the man. "*The harbour-master is attending to the arrival of one of the King's servants. I am one of his deputies, sir,*" he replied. "*May I enquire..?*"

"I am Gustavo Diego de Flores," Gustavo replied. *"See that no harm comes to my boat."* He turned to the rest of them. *"Come on, then. We haven't got all day."*

The port seemed busy with a newly-arrived boat, so they wandered away from the bustle until the sound of music called them into an inn. It was a waterfront place, with the sea and sky dominating half the world in front of it. From the doorway came a gentle breath of wine and tobacco.

Gustavo was first in, with John and Barnabas behind him. Christopher and Philip brought up the rear. They found a table in the corner where nobody else sat. Gustavo and Christopher sat at the ends of the benches, since their Spanish was good enough to pass as native speakers.

The band played a fast-paced folk dance of Spain. In front of them, in the middle of the room, three women were dancing. One was European, wearing a bright red dress and keeping time with castanets and the stamping of her boots. The other two were local girls, brown as she was pale and much younger than their leader. Their dance did not have the intricacy of the other, but they kept in step with exaggerated movements of their hips. The men watched and Christopher tried to make sure that the others noticed his own interest.

A man came over to them. *"Good evening, sirs,"* he said in accented Spanish, *"what can I offer you? We have wine, or beer."* He followed Christopher's gaze. *"Or perhaps you would like something else?"*

"Do you have a decent wine?" Gustavo asked. *"We do not want to pay for swill. Or for anything else that is an inferior copy of what we are used to back home."*

The waiter flinched when he heard Gustavo's Castilian accent. *"I am sorry, lord,"* he replied. *"We have a back room if you do not wish to be surrounded by peasants. A couple of the lady's men are there, but they are men of quality like you."*

"Which lady is this?"

"She is Our Lady Eva of Castile." the man replied. *"She arrived this morning."*

Christopher hoped his training in bedside manner would keep the shock off his face, but Gustavo's face did not show a flicker of response. *"I have no need to hear the boasts of military men either. Just bring a pitcher of decent wine and leave us alone."*

"Would you like any company?" he asked, glancing back at Christopher.

"No," said Gustavo. *"Just the wine. We don't want to be bothered. Don't you go gossiping about us either."*

"As you wish, lord," the man replied. He hurried away.

"What was that about?" Barnabas asked.

"She is here," Philip told him.

"In this inn?"

"Of course not. But she is in the town. That is all the commotion in the port: they are unloading her boat. Some of her bodyguard are in a back room."

"Perhaps we could question them," suggested John, grasping his fingers and cracking his knuckles.

"I think we would do better to keep our heads down," suggested Gustavo. "We are spies tonight, not fighters. Let us wait until the Drake Brothers put their plan into action. There will be plenty of time for fighting then."

"I have to make room for this wine," said Barnabas. He got up.

As he was standing the man returned with the pitcher of wine. He poured a little for Gustavo. *"How is it, lord?"*

"It will have to do," Gustavo replied, pulling a face. *"Now clear off."* The man hurried away.

"Do we have any idea how many she has brought?" Christopher asked.

"We could guess," John said. "Look around us. You can see the ones who are mercenaries."

"How many would a noblewoman normally travel with?" Philip asked.

"I don't know," Gustavo said. "In Spain she would only travel with a handful of men, but when I last met her she was accompanied by some of the finest fighting men the Order of St. James had to offer. And this is a land of savagery. She might travel with a hundred men for all we know."

"I don't see a hundred men," John said. "I don't see anyone that I would describe as 'finest fighting men' either."

"They might be in a private room, but I think they would have too much discipline to be drinking in a place like this. They will be crusader knights. They would be stationed wherever she is staying."

"Are they much threat?" Christopher asked. "Should we warn the Drake Brothers?"

"They are *crusader knights*, Christopher," Gustavo replied. "Crusader knights. Of course we should warn the Drake Brothers."

"Where is Barnabas?" asked Philip.

"He has been a long time," agreed John, "He had better not have fallen in."

They finished the wine and Gustavo left a réal on the table. They got up and went to look for Barnabas.

* * *

From the inn Barnabas walked through the town in the direction of the market square and the Governor's House. The Governor's House was easy enough to pick out, on the south side of the town's plaza. A broad verandah sheltered the door and, above it, many windows looked down on the market. Barnabas pretended to wander around the stalls looking at the produce, but it was those windows that really interested.

He saw one set of shutters open at the top of the Governor's House. The girl that reached out to secure them was brown, with black hair and a simple dress. Behind her Barnabas saw another woman, tall and elegant in bright silk. Her hair was a mass of tight blonde curls and her blue-green eyes looked down at the market a moment before they fell on Barnabas.

Looking up three storeys and across the length of the plaza Barnabas should have been hardly able to see her eyes, but the way her gaze held his was as if she was stood nose to nose with him. He stared up, rooted to the spot. He was aware that he shouldn't linger too long. He was aware that standing staring was not being inconspicuous at all. He would have to move on soon, but first he wanted to spend a few more moments looking up at her beautiful eyes.

Strong hands grabbed him and she looked away. As she turned from him the empty ache of rejection swept through his body, bringing tears to his eyes. He hardly noticed as they dragged him towards the Governor's House. He had stared upon the face of Aphrodite and she had spurned him.

— 6 —

The Queen of Pain

"When I find him I will kill him!" grumbled John, as they walked down yet another dark alley in Nombre de Dios. The locals were looking at them suspiciously.

"Hush, Master Overy," suggested Philip. "Not so loud."

"If you want to hear loud wait until I get my hands on him."

"We don't want to hear loud, Master John," suggested Gustavo, "Unless it happens to be in Spanish."

"Oh," answered John. "What is the Spanish for 'you fool'?"

"He might be in trouble," suggested Christopher.

"Not yet, he's not. But he will be."

Gustavo saw a group of men staring from a doorway. *"What are you looking at?"* he demanded in his grandfather's best accent.

"Nothing, sir," they replied.

By the time they were dragging him up the stairs Barnabas realised she had bewitched him. He tried to organise his own legs to carry him up the steps, but the soldiers that had taken him would not give him the space or the time to walk. They jostled and crowded him through the doors and pushed him onto the floor before her.

She looked down at him and spoke a moment in Spanish. The soldiers left, closing the door behind them. Then she whispered to herself. He recognised the Language of the Angels in her speech, crawling into the corners of his mind.

"Welcome," she said. He could not think of anything to say as she walked up to him and bent down a little. He felt like a small boy in the power of a great lady. She spoke again. *"I thought we should have a little chat, you and me."*

67

"Yes, mistress," he replied. The enchantment that had captured him was gone but, like the memory of a bad dream, the emotions remained. Every time he looked at her face the memory of it rose up.

"So," she said, *"Perhaps we should start with introductions. Today I am calling myself* Eva de Castilla."

"Today?"

"I have gone by many names," she replied. She waited a moment, then she went on. *"Let me show you a trick I learned when I was a girl."* Then she whispered more of those angel words and a silvery light, like the halo drawn around the Virgin in a Catholic painting, appeared around her head. She made a motion of grasping at thin air and a mirror appeared in her hand. She turned it so he could see his own reflection. He also had silvery light around his head.

"It's very pretty," he told her.

"Let me show you how it works," she answered. *"I am a dragon with two heads."* As she spoke, the light around her head darkened. *"Do you see what it does yet?"*

"It darkens when you tell an untruth?"

"You are a clever young Englishman," she smiled. *"Do you like my little trick? Did your master in England teach you a better one?"*

"None that I would show you, mistress," he answered. "You are very accomplished."

"This is a tiny trick."

"Your ability to make yourself understood is another trick, Mistress Eva. I hear you are not speaking my language but I can understand you anyway."

"Well done," she laughed. *"You really are a clever Englishman. But you still haven't told me your name. That's not very polite, is it?"*

"I am Barnabas Saul," he admitted.

"Now, Barnabas Saul, *let me show you another trick to help us get acquainted."* She went over to the door. "Maria?" she called. *"Where is* Maria?"

A moment later a girl hurried in. She was small and brown, in a dress that was threadbare in spots, and Barnabas could see the fear in her eyes. She spoke rapidly, a rattle of apologies in a language that he assumed was Spanish.

"Now, girl," she said to her servant, *"Now is a chance to make amends for your earlier failings. This nice Englishman is going to answer a few questions for me. If he tells the truth then I will be happy and inclined to forgive you. But if he doesn't tell the truth you can do me one last service, by showing him what I do to people who displease me."* The girl began

crying and babbling, and Eva snapped at her, *"Be quiet! Try and face death with dignity at least!"*

The girl quietened down, standing there whispering what Barnabas assumed to be prayers. Eva watched her a moment, openly enjoying the girl's terror. Then she sighed and turned to Barnabas. *"So,"* she asked, *"What is an Englishman doing in Nombre de Dios?"*

Barnabas knew he could not lie but he hoped he could avoid telling all the truth. "Gold," he replied, with as much sincerity as he could muster. "There is an enterprise to take the town and to steal the gold from your king's treasure house."

"How many?" she asked, as if she was asking about tomorrow's weather. *"And when?"*

"Tonight, mistress. There are about fifty of them."

She laughed. "Come to the window, Barnabas Saul."

He came over and she leaned gently on his arm. Her fragrance was strong in his nostrils and, remembering the enchantment by which he had been captured, he found his body stirring in response to her. Perhaps this was what the male spider felt when his mate was near, who would eat him as her wedding feast. She opened the shutter and directed his gaze down into the marketplace and the verandah of the Governor's House. His eyes came up to her neck and she made him feel like a child. She spoke again, laughter still in her voice. *"Do you see?"*

And he did see. Down in the square were many Spanish troops. Not colonists who had weapons, but regular Spanish troops, grim-faced men who did not smile or joke amongst themselves. They looked up to their mistress and gave their salute. She reached over his shoulder and drew the shutter again.

"There are one hundred and fifty soldiers here, my personal guard. They are veterans, they are loyal, and they will slaughter your silly English pirates without any trouble. This will be fine sport." She pressed his arm again, still gently. *"Would you like to stand here with me and watch it?"*

"I am in your power," he replied, knowing it to be true.

"I am glad you have realised so quickly," she replied. They walked back into the room, to where the terrified girl stood hoping they had forgotten her.

Eva hesitated, as if she had just remembered something. *"One other thing, Barnabas Saul. You mention your enterprise, but is that the only reason why your court magician should send his servant across the oceans? Is there another reason?"*

He looked uncomfortable for a moment, and the shine around his head flickered a little, but then came clear. "Yes, mistress. My master has asked me to gather information about navigation. He is interested in navigation, and has been for as long as I have been in his service."

"Of course. Navigation is the key to the oceans, and so to the world. And is there any other purpose?"

He looked more uncomfortable still.

"No, mistress, there is not."

The aura darkened around Barnabas' head. She looked over at the servant girl, who looked at Barnabas. He would not meet her gaze, since he had condemned her to death. The Lady swept her hand, as if she was gathering something from the air, then closed her fist, peered into the space within the closed hand and whispered something to the darkness. Then she stretched out the fist in front of her, towards the frightened servant, and squeezed. Barnabas caught a whiff of brimstone. The girl closed her eyes and the witch threw with her hand, throwing nothing at the servant.

As soon as that gesture was done, the girl started, even though fifteen feet separated the two and her eyes were closed. She looked shocked for a moment, then she screamed and fell to the floor, clutching at her stomach. Her screams continued for a moment and she thrashed around. Her belly was stretching, like an obscene parody of pregnancy, and there was a fizzing or sizzling sound. Her breath steamed in the air, as if it were cold, and the scream crackled a bit and then became quiet. Smoke began to pour from beneath her dress, and from her nose and mouth. She curled up a bit, and then lay still. The smell was terrible, the smell of burning flesh and humours that Barnabas knew from Tyburn, from when the entrails drawn from a living traitor were cast on the fire. The witch stared at the dying girl, searching at her face for signs of something. Then the girl breathed out, one last gasp that steamed in the warm air of the room, and she died.

The witch that called herself Eva of Castile called the servants in. *"Clear this mess up,"* she commanded.

The servants opened the shutters to let the smoke clear and began to clear away the mess.

The witch turned back to Barnabas. As she did so, he fought the urge to vomit.

"You see, Barnabas Saul, I am not like the fools that call themselves magicians in your home country. I am Queen of Atlantis and I have powers beyond any you can imagine. I have the power of death, and the power of eternal life. No mortal man can offer you the things that are in my gift. There is no reason at all for you to defend whatever mortal fool has sent you to oppose me."

Barnabas Saul did not answer. As he stared in horror at this terrible witch, he could still see the silver light around her head. As she spoke of immortality, the light remained pure and bright. She was telling the truth. He asked, just to be sure. "You could grant me immortality?"

She smiled and, for the first time since she had started to speak, he felt it was for him. *"So, you do have a price?"*

"Of course. Every man has a price, mistress," he replied. His aura also remained bright.

"If you find me the things I want, then maybe I will show you the secret of immortality." The servants looked at her, to check that she had no further interest in the corpse before they dragged it out. Barnabas Saul did not care anymore. He was going to live forever.

"Who is that?" asked Philip, turning into the alley.

"It's him," agreed Gustavo.

Christopher ran ahead and crouched down beside him. Barnabas was sat up behind some barrels. His clothes were torn and his face was bruised and bloody. "Barnabas, how are you?" Christopher asked.

Barnabas opened his eyes and grinned a bloody smile. "Uh wuh wuh," he said.

"What happened?" Christopher demanded.

"He's still acting the fool," growled John. "I'll get some answers out of him."

"He's hurt," said Christopher. "Leave him alone."

Barnabas spat blood. "I'm not that badly hurt. But if an Englishman wants to survive the city watch, he'd better be smart enough to act the fool. When they realised I was mute, they beat me and left me alone."

"Then you have had a lucky escape," said Philip. "You could easily have died a traitor's death."

"Some luck," Barnabas grumbled. He let Christopher help him to his feet and then he limped after them as they hurried back to their boat. He made very sure that none of them noticed the new dagger he had been given.

The Sun was setting behind them and the forest of the Spanish Main marched off the starboard side of the pinnace, a mile away. Barnabas had let Christopher bathe the cuts and bruises on his face with a rum-soaked rag, and had drunk a good measure of it afterwards. Gustavo had tried to help with the sail, since they were out of sight of land, but John saw straight away that he was no sailor. He knew it would be harder when it was full dark and that finding Drake and his men would be impossible. Meanwhile he and Christopher were handling the boat and the other three were sitting where they were told to and staying out of the way.

"Is that a sail?" asked Philip.

Behind them there was a single boat drawing away from the mouth of a river. They hadn't seen it when they passed, five minutes before.

"It is one of the pinnaces," answered John. "Get ready to go about!"

They got up and started to loose the sail. Then John heaved the tiller and the boat leaned over. The sail turned suddenly and the jib knocked Gustavo's hat off as it swept over their heads. Christopher and Philip caught the jib at the port side and made it fast. The canvas tightened. "Get over to the starboard side, you land-lovers!" he bellowed. "Blow your hat, Master Gustavo, if you don't want to get a ducking!"

The keel settled down and they began to make way through the swell. The pinnace turned around as they watched and returned into the river mouth, leading them on. "Where is that?" Philip asked. "Is that the Rio Francisco?"

"It must be," said John. "I don't have a chart but, unless we missed another river in this forest–"

"If it isn't then they have made the same mistake as we have," suggested Barnabas.

"I don't think Francis Drake would make that kind of mistake in navigation," said Christopher.

"He's only a young man," replied John. "It takes more than ambition to make a good navigator."

As the river-mouth opened around them they saw the three pinnaces, concealed behind some trees. John turned the boat in to follow them. As they got nearer he could see them men sitting about, waiting. "What kept you?" called Drake.

"Barnabas got caught. He didn't say anything. He pretended to be mute."

"Smart lad," said Drake. "But we need to get going. Come on," he shouted to the men, "Let's get under way."

"Don't you want to know what we found out?" asked Philip.

"Aye, lad," replied Drake. "We will be waiting all night to attack at dawn. There will be plenty of time to tell your tale."

* * *

By the time they had returned to the headland East of Nombre de Dios it was full dark. The Moon would not rise until midnight had passed, so there was nothing to compete with the glory of the tropical heavens. By starlight they dragged the boats ashore, knowing they were only a short distance from the eastward shore battery of the town. Above them, outlined against the sky, they could see the looming shape of the mountains of the Spanish Main. All around them was the unfamiliar sounds of the wildlife of that land, rustling, croaking and scraping their messages to the night.

The five companions dragged their own boat on shore then huddled together. They half-saw a couple of men come over and crouch beside them.

"So, Master Philip," Drake whispered, "Tell us what you have learned."

"There is a courtier in town," Philip replied. "She has a large company with her."

"She is a witch," interrupted Barnabas. "We should not be doing this."

"Why should I fear a witch?" asked Drake. "My faith is strong."

"You should fear this witch," Barnabas answered. "She has such mastery of the elements of nature that a whole army would be defeated by her alone."

"I hoped for some practical information about the city," replied Drake. "Master Philip, can you tell me anything useful?"

"She has a company of crusader knights, Captain," said Gustavo. "Knights of the Order of St. James."

"Now that is what I need to know. How many, and how are they armed?"

"We didn't see all of them," Gustavo shrugged.

"What about the King's men? Are any of them here?"

"King's men?" Gustavo scorned. "There will be some, I am sure. I am also sure we can discount them."

"I am sure we can't," growled John. "They are better disciplined than any band of knights."

"They are little better than mercenaries," sneered Gustavo. "There are no heroes among them."

"Mercenaries can be relied on to earn their wage," said Drake. "If we can frighten them they will run away, but if they think they have the upper hand then they will fight back."

Christopher didn't remember falling asleep but was suddenly awake, looking at the stars and shivering with cold. He got up to walk around and restore his circulation. He heard whisperings in the dark.

"... as big as Plymouth..."

"... a hundred armed men..."

"... Atlantean witch..."

He hurried back to find Francis. "Captain Drake," he whispered, "Wake up."

"What time is it?" Drake asked.

Christopher looked up the stars. The Moon had not yet risen but it silvered the horizon. "Three hours after midnight, I should say. Captain Drake, the men are frightened. They have another two or three hours until dawn but some of them are close to panic."

"What about? It's only a few Spaniards and none of them will dare to face my revenge. You will see."

"I don't doubt you, Captain Drake, not for a moment. But the men..."

"Then we will not give them any longer to wait, then," he said. He looked at the rising Moon. "That will be dawn enough for us."

The sentry peered out into the darkness. He knew that the Cimmarones were out there waiting for him, but it was so hard to stay awake. Then he heard a noise and he grabbed his weapon. *"Who is there?"* he called in Spanish.

He expected to see the savage faces of the Cimmarones but he certainly didn't expect to see three score armed Englishmen. He did not wait to talk. He ran away into the town, screaming. "The English are coming! The English are coming!"

The Englishmen gathered around the guns: six brass culverins pointing out over the water. John looked in the direction of the fleeing guard and shook his head.

"Shall we go after him, Captain?" one of the men asked.

"One Spaniard is not a problem," Drake replied. "These guns are the problem. Our boats will be slow when they carry the King of Spain's treasure. These will raise a hue and cry that we cannot afford to hear. There are more up there. They all need to be silenced." He picked out his best climbers and hurried off.

The rest of them waited, listening to the shouts from the town. Drums added their own urgent voices to the alarm.

"So much for surprise," grumbled Barnabas.

"The Captain is right," John replied. "We don't want those guns behind us when we retreat." The church bell began to ring, and Christopher saw all the men flinch at hearing that sound. John added, "It would be good if he didn't spend too long, though."

Although it was not long before Captain Drake returned, to the men waiting at the bottom of the hill it seemed like half the night had passed.

"What did you find?" John Drake called.

"There were no guns," Francis answered, "But there was a place ready for them. Brother, take Master Oxenham and another dozen men and go along the waterfront. If you come up the other side of the town we can come into the marketplace on two sides."

"Aye," agreed John Drake. "How will we know you are coming?"

"Go ahead. We will come up the hill with drums and trumpets. You go quietly ahead and attack when you hear us arrive."

"Come on, then," John Drake said to his men. Oxenham followed and the *Dragonfly's* crew went along with him. Barnabas looked back at the men guarding the boats but Oxenham urged him along.

They hurried along the waterfront. Occasionally they saw one of the inhabitants of Nombre de Dios, but they did not stay long. The braver ones threw something or, in one case, discharged a pistol, but none waited to argue the point. John Drake and John Oxenham led their men through the streets towards the marketplace.

"Stop," whispered John Overy. "Look at that."

They took cover among the buildings either side of the street. "What is it?" whispered John Drake.

"Look," said Philip. He pointed.

At the top of the street was the marketplace, but across the entrance they could see a row of bright red sparks.

"What are they?" Overy asked.

"They are the matches of guns," Barnabas whispered. "Can't you smell the fumes?"

"How many are there?" Oxenham asked.

"At least two dozen," Barnabas replied. "But... look at the way they move."

Christopher peered into the gloom. The apparently random motion of the lighted matches suddenly resolved itself into two waves of movement, passing along the line and back. It was almost as if the musketeers were dancing.

"They are on a couple of strings," Barnabas announced. "There are the matches of muskets but there are no musketeers."

As soon as he said it, the image became clear. The sparks were rolling around but they followed the curving lines of threads, being jiggled by some unseen hand.

Then they heard among the clamour of the town the sound of the drummers and the trumpeter. Then they heard the roar of muskets firing and the trumpeter was cut off mid-phrase. But the line of red sparks did not flash with fire. "Come on!" shouted Oxenham. "Our Captain's men are in the market square!"

They ran forward towards the line of sparks, shouting and yelling. They saw a figure run away from the end of the lights. As they burst into the market square they saw the English grappling with Spanish musketeers before the Governor's House. They fell upon their enemy from behind. Then, surrounded, the Spaniards broke away and ran back to the gate, and away along the royal road out of the city.

The brothers Drake greeted each other with hugs and slaps on the back. Francis was being followed by a lean brown man with a pike in his hand and a wicked grin on his face. "John, this is Diego. He believes we will be better masters than the Spanish."

"Welcome, friend Diego," replied John. "We should talk more, but first let us see if we can quiet those church bells."

But the church bells rang on. Francis sent men to try and stop it, but the church door was barred and there was no way in. The Governor's House was similarly barred: they could not even open a shutter. "The treasure house is down by the waterside," Francis told them. "Bar the city gate to keep the Spanish out and let us go down and load the pinnaces."

They counted their numbers as they returned to the shore. Only the trumpeter had fallen but there were a few who were hurt. Christopher looked the wounded men over and established that nobody was in danger before they walked back to the boats. As they reached the boats they heard a voice rise above the sound of the agitated town. At the sound of that voice the other sounds died away. Even the church bells fell silent.

The voice was a woman's voice, but the words that she called out sounded to the English as if a soloist had stepped forward to lead the plain-chants of Hell. Only the odd phrase drifted down as far as the waterside but each phrase drove every sane thought from their minds.

They all peered up at the town in the moonlight to see what was happening. Gustavo saw a figure standing on the church tower. She was waving her arms like a conductor and, a moment later, the Moon sailed behind a new cloud and was lost.

Christopher saw Gustavo and the way he reacted to the sight. He went over.

"It's her," Gustavo declared.

Christopher looked at the figure waving at the sky. A gust of wind blew down, rattling shutters and fluttering flags. Another snatch of her voice came down with it, inhuman words carried on the wind.

"You can't tell at this distance," Christopher said after a moment.

"It is her," repeated Gustavo.

Philip came up to Christopher and Gustavo. "What are you looking at?" he asked.

Gustavo pointed.

"She is making weather," Christopher replied.

Philip looked at Gustavo. "You said she would be in Spain," he said. "You said the King of Spain had forbidden women to travel to the New World."

"Not without their husbands," Gustavo replied, remembering the last time he had spoken to her. "Maybe she got married."

"Or maybe she cares nothing for the King's laws," added Christopher.

"Are you taking her seriously now?" Gustavo asked Philip.

"I heard of witchcraft," Philip replied, "But I never really believed it before tonight."

The clouds were marching across the sky, swirling around the Governor's House. Like the conductor at the crescendo she flung her arms up, and the clouds responded with a volley of lightning. The flashes punctuated the movement around them in jerky images.

Philip looked around but Christopher watched the rain like a curtain sweeping down the hill. Barnabas stood in the flickering light, his face contorted with anger or fear.

"Get under cover!" Captain Drake shouted. "*Run!*" His words seemed to break through the hypnotic effect of the witch's chant and the men ran towards the treasure house. At the end of it there was a covered shade and they made for that. But they were only half-way when the storm swept over them. The drops felt like warm hail, bouncing off the stones as high as their knees. Through the rain they could hardly see the treasure house.

Lightning illuminated the men as they gathered in the shelter. Christopher found a light and looked at some of the wounded men. He could not do much but he could make bandages to staunch blood. The wounds seemed very light given that they had absorbed a whole volley of musket fire. But he kept his suspicions to himself and kept working.

John Overy wandered off somewhere with Gustavo following. Nobody wanted to go out and follow them into the rain, even if their guns and bows were so thoroughly soaked that the rain could make no difference.

But after half an hour the storm passed as suddenly as it had arrived. Captain Drake led them around to the front of the treasure house. The men tried the door. They rattled it and shook it but it would not yield.

"It's locked," Barnabas grumbled.

"And here are John and Gustavo with the key!" replied Captain Drake.

They all looked around. Overy was leading, with his arms wrapped around a tree-trunk. Gustavo and Philip between them had the back on their shoulders. The men gave a cheer and many hands grabbed the huge chunk of wood. They carried it over to the door.

They gathered around it, the strongest six on each side, and swung it into the door. Feet slithered on the wet stones as they heaved with all their strength. The sound was deafening and Gustavo looked up the hill towards the Governor's House, sure there would be a counterattack. The first impact was a boom, but the second carried a sound of splintering wood. They took that as encouragement and drove it all the harder, running up to the door and smashing the tree trunk close to where the latch must be.

But Gustavo wasn't watching them. He was looking up to the church, trying to catch a glimpse of his enemy.

Crash! went the door as their improvised battering ram hammered into it. Then one door twisted on its hinge and hung open. The men surged in with shouts and screams and Barnabas followed.

The darkness was dispelled a little by one or two lanterns. At one end of the vaulted space there was a few small chests, but there was a much larger empty space where the treasure had been stored.

"Empty! It's gone!" Barnabas screamed. "The treasure fleet has come and gone!"

Captain Drake looked around his bedraggled and disheartened band. He drew his sword. "To the Governor's House!" he shouted. "There will be gold there!" When the men did not respond as quickly as he would have liked, he added, "I have brought you to the treasure house of the world. If you leave empty-handed you have no-one to blame but yourselves!"

That did it. His words lifted their heads and they followed him out into the dying rain. The moon came out again as they followed him up. But as he ran he stumbled and fell. He did not get up as the men gathered around him.

The South Sea

"Let me through!" Christopher ordered, in a voice that surprised Philip. They made way for him. Christopher knelt beside him. "Captain Drake, open your eyes," he ordered. When he got no response he turned Drake onto his back and opened his mouth. Drake was still breathing but they could see in the moonlight that one of his legs was darkened with blood. Christopher found a bottle in his bag, popped off the cork and cradled Drake's head in his arm. With the other hand he opened Drake's mouth and poured in the mixture.

Drake spluttered and his eyes opened. "Come on," he said, trying to get to his feet.

"There will be other days for gathering Spanish gold, Captain," Christopher told him. "Today you need a surgeon to attend to your leg. You have lost a lot of blood and you do not have the strength for the fight." He looked around the others as he tied a strip of cloth tightly above Francis' knee. "Gentlemen," he said, "Who will help carry our captain to the boats?"

Strong arms lifted him to his feet and supported him as Oxenham led them back to the pinnaces. The rain had stopped and the wind was no more than a breeze as they sailed across the harbour. Gustavo was not sure who had given the order but all four boats were pointed at the Spanish merchantman. As they got closer they could see nobody on deck. Men climbed quickly on board and found just five Spaniards, who showed with open palms that they were unarmed.

As soon as the pinnaces were secured the English spread the sails of their prize and turned for the island beyond the bay. One of the guns of the shore battery fired, but they didn't even see where the shot landed. It did not hinder their escape but, even if the night had not been the success they had hoped for, they were not going empty-handed.

"Captain Drake! Captain Drake!" one of the men shouted, "Come and see what we have found in the aft cabin!"

"Where is he?" Eva screamed. "I want him here now!"

The governor ran up to her door. "I am here, Our Lady," he called.

She opened the door. He looked up at her and saw the anger in her face. "What have you done with my ship?" she demanded.

"The English—"

"You fool! You knew they were coming. I told you yesterday. How could you let them steal my ship?"

"But, Our Lady, you told the men to fall back."

"I didn't tell them to give my ship away!"

"We can get you another ship, Our Lady."

"Will this other ship have all my papers in it?"

"Your papers, Our Lady?"

"My papers. My researches. Eighty years of news from the New World."

"Will the English understand it?"

"Of course not. My notes are taken in my own language. I am the last of us in Europe. I killed my last rival more than seven hundred years ago."

"Then I will go to the English and ask for them to return your papers, Our Lady. They will not be able to understand them so they will have no use for them. I will offer them gold. Englishmen always want gold."

"You make sure that you get them back," she warned, "Or Nombre de Dios will have a new governor."

Christopher Stoke ordered the men to put Captain Drake in the cot in the captain's cabin. Surprisingly, the captain's cabin wasn't the largest, and they had to squeeze around the chart table. He sat on a stool beside the cot and carefully took Drake's boot off. As he put the boot down he heard something fall on the wooden floor. He bent down and picked it up. It was a musket ball, flattened on one side where it had hit something hard. He handed it to Drake and then looked back at the wound.

"I may be able to ease the pain with a form of prayer, Captain," he explained. "But you will have to trust me."

"I have no objection to hearing your prayer, Doctor Stoke," Francis replied.

"Then close your eyes and we will begin."

Drake closed his eyes and Stoke began the process, adapting the words he was using to make them sound suitably prayerful. But the leg in his hands would not take on the characteristic muscle tone. "I am sorry, Captain, but it seems your will is too strong for my art. You will have to endure my pokings and proddings, I am afraid."

Captain Drake shrugged. "Then do your worst, friend surgeon," he replied.

Stoke prodded around, acutely aware from listening to his patients breathing that he was hurting. He tried to be gentle as he explored the wound. The bones seemed to be untouched, thankfully, and the foot seemed still to have good circulation and mobility. He cleaned the wound and sterilised it as best he could, then stitched it up. He stood up then lifted the stool onto the cot, to prop the leg up.

"You will have to stay like that for a few hours, Captain. You have lost a lot of blood and you can ill afford to lose more. I will come and see how you are doing in a little while. If the wound drains well and the inflammation subsides then you can get up."

"I am not accustomed to being a prisoner, doctor," Drake said.

"Doctor's orders, Captain," Stoke replied.

John Overy stood at the wheel. Beside him was Diego, the slave that Captain Drake had freed from the Spanish. "Make for that island," Diego pointed. "There is food and drink there."

"You are not, perhaps, a pilot?" asked John.

"No," Diego replied.

"Pity." John looked up and shouted. "Hey lads, get ready to turn to port. You and you, get up and into the tops. And Mark Tanner, see if you can find a plumb line. We will need it if we are not to run aground."

"Aye," they shouted, and rushed to comply. When he saw that they were ready at the sails, he turned the wheel. Their new prize heeled over a little and the lads clumsily re-set the sails. The boat seemed to drift sideways somewhat and he turned the wheel a little more to make sure they would arrive at their destination, for all it was to one side of the prow. "I miss the boats of the Hawkins Brothers," he told anyone who would listen. "This is like trying to ride an ox, when one is accustomed to the finest thoroughbred horse."

"We have twenty fathoms clear," Mark's voice sang out from the bows.

"Good lad!" shouted John. "Keep calling them."

With Mark calling the depths and the smallest amount of sail, they found a bit of shelter and a wooden dock reaching out into the water. They made their new prize fast and went ashore. The island was given over to fields and livestock. A few peasants quickly surrendered, and John ordered a cask of wine from the ship's cargo opened.

Christopher opened the door of the other cabin. Barnabas was sitting in front of a writing desk, with books and papers scattered around. "What have you got?" Christopher asked.

"There are papers," he said. "Letters and books." He shuffled through the papers and selected a letter. "This one is from one Francisco de Toledo to an Eva de Castilla."

"Gustavo's Eva?"

"It sounds like it." Barnabas scanned through. "Listen. '*I regret to inform you that I still have not found the gods of these strange people. We know that their gods are tall with fair skin and blue eyes. But all they will tell us of this hidden god is that he left by walking over the sea. They won't tell us where to find him.*' It goes on to say..." Barnabas followed the Latin with his finger. "... here it is. '*Even under the hard and long pain they refuse to tell us where to find the golden prize you seek. There is nothing more that can be done...*' What do you think they are looking for, doctor?"

"It is clear enough what they are looking for. They are looking for the same thing we are looking for. But are we sure it is Gustavo's Eva we saw last night, soaking us with her control of the weather?"

Barnabas pushed another letter over. "Have a look at this."

Christopher quickly scanned it. "It gives Eva of Castile permission to travel to the New World and provides for her a royal guard. That matches Gustavo's story. What about the books?"

"Most of the books are in Latin but they are annotated. This one, though, is in the language that annotates the rest." He turned to Christopher and offered a book. Christopher opened it. The writing was done with a quill, small flowing characters lined along the page. As soon as he saw it Christopher knew it was her.

"Can you read that?" Barnabas asked.

"They are pictures," Christopher replied. "Look, this is a fish and that looks like the snout of a pig. That is the ocean and this is an island. There is a bird in flight and–"

"I can see that," said Barnabas. "They say the writing of Aegypt is like this."

"That is not Egyptian," answered Christopher. "The symbols of Egyptian hieroglyphics are grouped in rectangular formations. These are in a row, like the Latin characters we use."

"Hiero-glyphics?" asked Barnabas.

"Priest writing. The writing is supposed to be engraved on their temples and carved idols."

"Well, if this is not the script of Aegypt, what is it then? Is it Atlantean?"

"It must be."

"Then what does this symbol show?" He was pointing to a symbol of an eye at the top of a triangle.

"It sounds to me like it shows pure witchcraft," suggested Captain Drake, leaning in the doorway.

"Is Greek or Latin witchcraft?" asked Barnabas. "Learned men read in the languages of the ancients to learn the science they knew. The Greeks lived in a golden age of reason: their philosophies exceeded anything we have today. According to Platon the Atlanteans lived ten thousand years earlier. What philosophies are contained in this book?"

"There is one book that can provide all the philosophy one man might need," replied Francis.

"The Queen knows her Greek," said Christopher.

"In order that she can read the Bible in the original tongue," replied Francis.

"Anyway," said Christopher, "You should be resting that leg. You have sustained a serious injury and lost a lot of blood."

"Spare us from all physicians!" exclaimed Captain Drake. But he limped away.

"You should get Philip and Gustavo," said Christopher. "Most of these books are written in Latin."

"I know my Latin."

"I never said you didn't. But two heads are better than one, Barnabas Saul, and we may not have these in our hands for very long. Francis Drake thinks he is our captain but he doesn't see the value in these books. We should learn what we can, while we still can."

Barnabas hurried off and Christopher opened one of the Latin books, hoping to skim it and learn from the annotations. He saw the frontpiece, and saw a dedication written by hand. It was from the author, Pedro Cieza de León, to his patron, Joanna, Princess of Asturias – Queen of all Spain.

* * *

"Captain Drake," cried one of the men, "There's a sail!"

Drake limped out onto the deck and Christopher shook his head then followed.

The sail was a little boat: what the English might have called a pinnace. Half a dozen Spanish seamen sat around a lone soldier. They found their way over the water to where Drake's pinnaces were moored around the prize ship. He called out in Latin. *"Hail! I come to you willingly, wishing to parley."*

Captain Drake looked at Christopher. "Is that Spanish?" he asked.

"No, Captain, it is Latin."

"Well, tell him he may come aboard. If he offers no violence he will leave unharmed."

Christopher made the translation into Spanish and then translated the reply back into English.

"I was afraid you were French. Although you English steal the King's ships and gold, you are not cruel. But the governor sent me with two questions and a request."

"Well," said Drake, "Since we are your guests, it seems, ask your questions and make your request. But first, join us for dinner."

Captain Drake commanded that his men set out a table for them to eat and, with a bit of searching around, silverware was found on the ship to set the table with. The old soldier sat down and, when the food was brought out, they began to eat.

"So," Captain Drake asked, "What are your questions?"

Christopher listened to the Spanish soldier speak. *"The first question is about you, Captain. May we know the name of our guest?"*

"Well, sir," Captain Drake replied when Christopher had translated, "I am Francis Drake. I was commander of the *Judith* when Martín Enríquez gave and then broke his word to us. We lost a ship and many men that day, and I am here claiming my just compensation for such treachery."

Christopher looked at the Spanish soldier. *"Captain Drake says that he feels justified in taking the King's gold since the King's governor broke truce with him at San Juan de Ulúa four years ago. I am sure that is not the way that you have heard it, though."*

"It is certainly not," replied the soldier, *"But I do not wish to contend the point. I was given other orders."*

"Of course," agreed Christopher. *"What is your other question?"*

"The second question is about your arrows. Are they poisoned?"

"No!" exclaimed Drake when Christopher had translated. "Of course not. Tell your surgeons that no special treatment is needed."

Christopher told him, adding that soaking the wound with brandy before closing it would help the wound to heal without infection. Then he asked, *"And what was the request?"*

"Well," began the soldier, *"It seems that there was a passenger on this ship, a lady from King Philip's court. The ship was newly arrived, and her luggage was not fully unloaded."*

Christopher looked at Captain Drake. "This man is asking for the witch's luggage," he explained.

"I have told you that I care nothing for tales of witches," Captain Drake replied.

"Surely, Captain," interrupted Gustavo, "You remember that storm that left us unable to fight this morning."

"I have seen weather change very fast in these latitudes," Captain Drake replied. "Tell him that we will return the lady's chest to her."

"Now wait a moment," said Barnabas.

"No, I will not hear any more of your sorcerous chatter, Master Saul. It is not noble for a gentleman to deprive a lady of her personal effects, especially so far from civilisation. Even if she is Spanish and Catholic, we are still decent men."

"Do decent men keep their word, Captain Drake?" asked Christopher.

"Of course," he replied. "What of it?"

"You promised our Captain Ranse that he should have the first pick from the booty that we took from the raid, and that you should dispose of the rest as you saw fit."

"You may have the hands of a healer, Doctor Stoke, but..." Drake turned to John Overy. "John, do you think your master would support this ill-mannered demand?"

Philip spoke up. "Normally I would agree with you, Captain Drake, but today I must take their part. We have our orders, from Lord Burghley himself."

"Surely Lord Burghley's orders do not extend to plundering a lady's luggage?"

"In this particular case, they do."

Drake glowered at them. "I know William and John Hawkins very well, young Master Sidney. When I return to England I will ask them to inquire with Lord Burghley. You would not want me for an enemy."

"I must apologise for that," replied Philip, "But I must serve my queen."

"Very well," conceded Drake. "Fetch her chest. You may remove one item."

"Take the diary," whispered Christopher to Barnabas.

"Which one is the diary?" he whispered back.

"It is the one which is hand-written in Atlantean, of course."

They stayed on the islands outside Nombre de Dios for three days, by which time Captain Drake and most of his wounded men were well on the way to recovery. They sailed East again, until they met Ranse with the three ships.

The two captains and their companies greeted one another cheerfully enough, but Christopher took Captain Ranse aside. Philip and Gustavo followed them into Ranse's cabin, with Barnabas trailing behind. John Overy was already waiting in the cabin. "Shut the door," said Ranse.

Christopher shut the door. "Captain Ranse," Gustavo explained, "She is in Nombre de Dios. We got her diary."

"Captain Drake isn't happy about that," added Christopher.

"There is bound to be important information in that diary," suggested Barnabas.

"If anyone can read it," said Gustavo. "To me it looks like a child has drawn a load of pictures."

"Captain Drake does not recognise that she is dangerous," Christopher said. "He just thinks we are stealing a book from a woman."

"I would suggest that book contains State secrets," said Philip.

"Do we think it does?" asked Captain Ranse.

"I think it does," said Barnabas, "If only we had the key to that code."

"I am sure it does," said Christopher. "Lord Burghley would want access to it – and would be disappointed if he were to hear that it slipped through his fingers."

"I doubt your fellowship with Captain Drake will survive," said John. "He was very unhappy."

"He did promise us the first choice of any booty," said Christopher.

"But he doesn't understand why we consider the lady's diary to be booty," argued John.

"Well," said Captain Ranse, "We demanded first choice because we knew our first loyalty was to Edward Horsey and to Lord Burghley. We knew there might be hard choices. Here we are. Captain Drake will just have to take it to Lord Burghley if he is unhappy."

* * *

When they had taken their leave of John Oxenham and the Brothers Drake, Captain Ranse took the *Dragonfly* out of the bay and along the coast. They were looking for the Cimmarones - the wild men who so bitterly opposed their Spanish enemies. Diego promised Christopher that, if he went to a particular inlet and mentioned Diego's name, the Cimmarone King who lived there would offer help.

James Ranse and John Overy stood on the quarterdeck of the *Dragonfly* and looked out at the forest that came right down to the sea. John was holding the wheel and James was pacing about. The *Dragonfly* was only under a little sail as they drifted before the wind, up the river. The tide was about to turn and James knew that, if they had to escape in the next few hours, they could rely on the currents to take them back out to sea.

"Do you trust them?" asked John Overy.

"No more than I trust the Spanish," replied Captain Ranse.

"There is that," agreed John. "So now what?"

"I'm not going to wait while the tide turns. Get the men to load a gun with no ball and fire it. That should tell them that we are here."

The men hastened to comply and the sound of the shot roared like thunder. From all the trees along the waterside birds took flight, whirring around the inlet. "Well, they know we are here now," said John.

Captain Ranse extended his spyglass and peered along the coast. "I think I see them," he said. "Tell the men to get the boat ready. We will send our young bravos out and see what happens."

"Should I go?"

"Do you want to come back with more spines than a hedge-hog?"

"Probably not. But I should go anyway."

They rowed towards the shore. This time Gustavo sat beside Philip and Christopher beside John, with Barnabas sitting and watching. Four more men from the *Dragonfly*'s crew rowed behind them.

"I see them," announced Barnabas.

"How do they look?" asked Christopher.

"They look well armed," Barnabas said. "I see spears."

They kept rowing, even if they were waiting for arrows or spears between their shoulder-blades. The boat bumped on the bottom and Gustavo and Christopher sprang out. Christopher spoke in Spanish. *"Friends,"* he said, *"Will you talk to us? We have gifts."* He was relieved to see a few smiles.

They made gifts of glass beads and iron nails, noting that it was the iron that seemed more welcome. One of the Cimmarones came forward. *"I heard about Captain Drake and the raid on Nombre de Dios,"* he said. *"It made us laugh to see the Spanish running out of their own gate."*

"We have another plan for the Spanish," explained Gustavo. *"We want to go over the mountains to the other port, and steal a ship. We mean to sail the South Seas."*

"Would you guide us there and help us back when we return?" asked Christopher.

"Yes," they agreed. *"We will."*

So it was that, a day later, Philip, Gustavo, Christopher, John, Barnabas and a dozen of the *Dragonfly's* crew were walking down towards the port of Panama with the Cimmarones as porters and scouts. Panama was a simple town, more active than Nombre de Dios, established the year around, not crowded only when the gold came. The Cimmarones pointed out the *Camino Réal*, the road that was used to carry the gold, but they were careful to stay off it. The shelter of the trees hid them from Spanish eyes and that was what they wanted. They knew that messengers would have brought news of Captain Drake's raid on Nombre de Dios and it seemed too risky to use the road.

John looked down with his spy-glass. "The town is walled by a wooden palisade," he explained, "but I see no shore batteries and no defences around the harbour. There is some newly-constructed boat being loaded with provisions. They are loading the water, so they must expect to go in a day or so."

"Do you see many crew?" asked Philip.

"Only two men," John replied. "There might be more below decks, of course. But I think they are expecting the ship to sail when the crew arrive."

John put the spyglass down and looked at the rest of them. He saw the same expression on all four faces.

"It's her boat," said Gustavo.

"We should take it," added Philip.

"It would make sense," agreed Christopher. "Without a boat she will be delayed."

"We should wait for dark," said Barnabas.

It was dusk as they approached the gate of Panama. Gustavo led the way. He strode up to the gate and thought of how his grandfather would have spoken. "Boy, where is the good inn at this town?"

The guard stepped aside. "Sir, there is good accommodation at the Sign of the Golden Monkey."

Gustavo imagined what his grandfather would say. "And which relative of yours runs the place?"

The guard was embarrassed as he admitted, "My cousin owns it, but that is how I know it is good. Tell him that Jose sent you, and he will take good care of you."

Gustavo walked past the way his grandfather used to walk and the Englishmen silently hurried to keep up. They were in Panama.

Once in the narrow streets they walked down towards the waterfront. They were vaguely following the directions to the inn, but the waterfront was also where the boats could be found. Most of the people who earlier had been working on the boats were making their way to the inns. Saul spotted a brown-skinned girl in a European dancing gown, faded and too big for her. A man watched her from the alley behind. As the light faded, they recognised the boat they were planning to steal. None of them pointed it out, or slowed their pace, but they tried to take in as much detail as they could.

"Now we need a distraction," suggested John.

"Wait here," said Saul. "I have just the thing."

"You remember what happened at Nombre de Dios?" Philip warned.

"Trust me," replied Saul. And, before any of them could object, he hurried off into the darkness.

"What do you think he's up to this time?" asked Philip suspiciously.

"No good, I'm sure," John replied. "I don't know why Captain Ranse allowed him on the voyage. He's a witch, that's for sure. Witch is wicked – and bad luck too. All the crew know it and it doesn't do their courage any good. If he doesn't–"

But they never heard what it was that he should or should not do. There was a thump they felt rather than heard then, with a roar, a huge cloud of red flame billowed out over the roofs. A building on the waterfront had exploded.

"The magazine," suggested Philip.

"It happens sometimes," replied John, "Especially if people are careless. Too many people smoking that vile weed."

Whatever John thought of the weed, it was a fine distraction. People were running down the dock and the two men left to guard the boat were leaning over the deck, craning their necks to see what was occurring. It was too easy. With all the shouts and noise, they didn't hear John and Philip running up the plank. John grabbed one pair of ankles and tipped him over the side. Philip took the other's arm, twisted it around in some wrestling style, and the other guard followed his companion over the rail and into the water. Gustavo was cutting the rope that held the ship to the dock and the crew were setting the sail to catch the night breeze when Saul came running up the gangplank. He was out of breath and smelt faintly of sulphur.

The two that they had pitched into the water were clambering out and trying to raise the alarm but, with the shouting about the explosion and in the half-light, they could make themselves understood neither with voices or gestures. The sails were up and catching the night wind and the dock was moving away astern.

Saul waved them goodbye and one of them shook his fist in rage.

— 8 —

The Temple and the Star

Above them was a vault of clear blue. The Sun glared down at them and the ocean reflected the brightness back up. A lazy wind was enough to fill the sails but hardly to raise a wake. John leaned on the port-side rail and fiddled with his spy-glass. Beyond them, the Western horizon had a dirty smudge that John knew was this parched land.

Christopher came up to join him. "What do you see?" he asked.

"See for yourself," replied John, offering the spy-glass.

Christopher extended the brass tubes and steadied his elbows on the rail. He bent down to put his eye to the thin end. John looked down as his companion leaned forward.

"There is smoke," said Christopher.

"Ciudad de los Reyes," replied John. "The charts show a large town."

"We can't land there," said Christopher. "If news has come from Nombre de Dios they will be looking for us."

"But we must land soon," replied John. "We have had no water since yesterday."

"We can manage a little longer," said Christopher. "Even in this heat none of us are showing signs of dehydration yet. Perhaps we could put in at nightfall."

"Put in?" asked John. "Put in where?"

Christopher scanned the horizon with the spy-glass. "I think there is a river mouth there. Perhaps if we made our way up the river a way it would–"

John leaned over and took the spyglass. He scanned up and down the horizon a couple of times before he found it. "It could be a river mouth," he agreed. "It's not on the charts. But we could take a little risk, I would think." He noted various landmarks, measuring the angles from the boat with his hand at arm's length. "We will come back at dusk. The tide will be out so, if we are careful, we can recover from a grounding."

* * *

It was easy enough to return even after night had come. John had the positions of the mountain peaks on the horizon committed to memory, so he was able to pilot them in. With only a little sail they soon found themselves anchored in the river's stream. But, however thirsty they were, he would not allow them to go ashore until daybreak.

So, after feverish dreams, they came ashore in a little boat. The land was scrubby and neglected. Barnabas wandered off, but the rest of them concentrated on filling the barrels.

They were lifting the barrels back on to the boat when Barnabas came running back down the bank. "Pyramids!" he shouted. "There's pyramids!"

Gustavo looked at Philip. "*Santa Cruz!*" he swore, "What is that crazy man shouting about now?"

"He has been talking about pyramids since before we landed," Christopher reminded them. "He said, 'Find me pyramids and I will find your treasure'."

"We should go and look," said Philip.

"Can you men finish filling these barrels and get them back on the boat?" John asked the crew. "We will be back soon. Make sure you don't knock them. We are short enough of water already on this arid coast without leaky barrels."

"Aye," the men replied.

They scrambled up the dusty bank, through the thorn bushes, following Barnabas' lead. John brought up the rear, sweating in the heat.

Philip was the first to see. Above the bank they saw pyramids of mud brick, baked hard like stone in the desert heat. Between them and the pyramids they saw other buildings constructed to a more human scale. Everything looked abandoned, with the desert plants growing right up to doorways and through the gaping windows. But Barnabas stopped and pointed. "Look at this, lads," he said.

It was a footprint, toes visible in the dust. The footprint was smaller than any of theirs.

"Is it a child?" Philip asked.

"No," said Christopher. "Look at the angle of the big toe and the way the weight is placed. This is not a child's footprint. It is an old person's footprint. I would guess it is a woman of forty or fifty years."

"You can tell all that from looking at a mark in the dirt?" John asked scornfully.

"A footprint is the mark left by the way we walk," Christopher replied. "A child walks like this," he said, taking a few steps bouncing on his toes. "But this person walked like this." His shoulders slumped forward and his footsteps were shuffling. "A woman places her feet ahead of each other in a line, but a man places his feet either side of a line."

John looked at the way Christopher's hip swayed when he walked like a woman. "I wonder if that comes more naturally to you than–"

"That is hardly a seemly thought, Master Overy," admonished Philip.

"Oh, I'm used to it," laughed Christopher. "John has been away from civilisation so long he has forgotten what a real woman looks like. That is an old woman's footprint. We should find her. She might be able to tell us something."

Barnabas looked around and then spoke in his strange voice. "This temple has kept its power," he said. "There must be priests here."

"Pagan priests," scorned John.

They split up and worked their way around the smaller buildings. Christopher and Gustavo were working their way along the left, further away from the river, while Philip and John worked their way along the right.

"Do you believe any of this stuff?" asked Gustavo.

"What do you mean?" Christopher asked.

"You are a learned man, Doctor Stoke. You must have seen the beginnings and ends of life. Do you think God dwells in churches?"

"I am sure He does," Christopher replied. "Other places too."

"*She* told me that religion was the way they controlled us."

"*She* didn't build this temple, did she? It is a part of human nature to seek after the divine and to find ways to honour it. We all..."

Christopher noticed the way Gustavo's body froze and he stopped speaking. Gustavo was looking at an open doorway. "I saw something," he whispered. His hand strayed down to his sword.

They stood still a moment, but Christopher glanced down reproachfully at Gustavo's hand and he left the sword in its scabbard. Then Christopher saw the movement in the shadow of the doorway again. He slightly nodded his head and Gustavo responded. He had seen it too.

The doorway they were standing before was as overgrown as the others, with a dried-out thorn bush blocking the entrance. But when Gustavo carefully pulled the branches the whole bush came away. It was not rooted. He crept over the threshold.

The movement came again. He whirled around, pulling his sword out and stabbing it at the movement. Out of the shadows ran a small lizard, its toes sticking to the brick. It scuttled up around the lintel and out of reach, under the roof. It glared down at them with a bright eye.

Gustavo laughed. "Be careful, my little friend. If you surprise armed men like that, some day you will lose your pretty tail."

Christopher smiled back. "It's the silence. It puts us on edge."

Gustavo nodded as he put his sword back. "Sometimes silence can be worse than the shouts of battle. Remember Nombre de Dios, when we were waiting for the Sun to rise?"

Christopher did not see what happened next. Hands appeared and grabbed Gustavo's hair. Christopher saw the flash of metal. Then Gustavo staggered back out of sight. Christopher ran forward to help but his feet tangled in the thorn-bush. He entered the melée face-first.

There was a struggle of limbs. Something bright and metallic pounded Christopher's chest-plate with dull clangs. A fist caught him on the side of his head, filling the darkness with stars. Then he heard a woman's voice shout. "*Stop*," cried Christoper in Spanish. "*We need to question her.*"

"She's not going anywhere," Gustavo grunted out of the darkness.

The woman screamed at Gustavo in her tongue.

"Let her go," said Christopher. Then he breathed in and tried to remember how to reply. He spoke a moment and the woman let Gustavo go.

Christopher found his feet and led Gustavo out. The old woman followed them. She was short, with long iron-grey hair in a plait. She wore a cloak and tunic which must have been brightly coloured once, but now were faded and worn. She looked them up and down disdainfully and demanded a question of them.

Christopher spoke with her a moment, made their apologies and their introductions.

"You speak that barbarous tongue?" Gustavo asked. "What is she saying?"

"She is telling me that she is the priestess. I asked her name."

"What is her name?"

Christopher smiled, confident that Gustavo would not have understood one word she had said. "She says to call her *Palla*," he answered.

Francisco de Toledo was sitting at his writing desk, reading a report from one of his officers. Suddenly his body stiffened slightly and he reached for his bag. He glanced around to make sure the servants had left and he took out a small dagger. Around the hilt of the dagger he saw a pattern of light. He put his hand over the light.

"*Dona* Eva," he whispered.

how are your searches going the words of his mistress replied.

"As well as we can, Our Lady," he whispered. "This is very rough country and the natives do not offer any clues. They defy me and–"

your methods are crude and ineffective francisco

"I am utmostly sorry, Our Lady."

now there is a new thing for you to find came her reply. *there are english pirates that have stolen a boat in the south sea and are coming to find it*

"How many?"

a score or more

"They are all English?"

there is one spaniard among them

"Then they will be easy enough to find, Our Lady."

make sure you find them her words replied. *i am coming to cuzco and i will show you the right way to interrogate someone*

"I am sorry the king said nothing."

i have given you another chance don francisco she replied. *one more chance is all you will get*

They met by the side of the river. The priestess agreed to accompany Christopher. He could sense her reluctance, but he could also sense her loneliness.

"This is Palla," said Christopher. She smiled as she heard her title and Christopher continued. "She is the last priestess of this temple, apparently."

Barnabas was the first to respond. "Get her to tell us about her temple and her god."

Christopher turned to the priestess. He spoke to her and listened to her reply. Then he switched to English. "She says she serves a hidden god called *Kon Tiki*, who taught people how to be civilised."

"Tell her to tell us where we can find this *Kon Tiki*," said Barnabas. They listened while Christopher spoke to the priestess with barely-concealed impatience.

"What is all this chatter?" John broke in. "Can she help us or not?"

"She might be able to," Christopher replied. "I am trying to negotiate her services."

"Let him be," said Philip.

"Yes, John, let him be," added Barnabas. "There is more to this matter than counting barrels and lashing crew."

"I'll lash you, Barnabas Saul–"

"Do we need to do this now?" asked Philip.

Christopher apologised to the priestess and then continued the conversation. Finally he turned to the others. "Palla says she has a list of tasks that need to be completed before she can leave the temple. If we help her complete the tasks so she can leave her office here then she will spend a year and a day helping us to find her *Kon Tiki*."

"Let us see the list of things she needs," Philip replied. "If the list does not contain any unpleasant surprises, we will do it. Tell her."

Christopher told her.

Christopher looked up from the campfire. His companions were drinking their rum ration and the talk had become rather more loud and pointless. He knew he would not be missed. He got up and gathered his cloak around him. The stars gave a little light but he wished he had a proper torch. "Now," he thought to himself, "If I was an old priestess whose temple had been invaded by drunken English tourists, where would I go? Where would I hide?"

He walked up to the barracks where they had first found her. In the cool evening, among the sounds of the insects, he could hear someone singing. The tune was unfamiliar to Christopher but, for all that, he suspected the singer was slightly off-key. It certainly sounded off-key to him.

He found her sitting in one of the rooms. She had corn porridge steaming in a bowl but she was singing to herself instead of eating. He could hear the words. She was singing to Mother Earth, then to her son. The song to her son was a song of praise, but Christopher could hear her singing it like a love-song. He waited patiently while she finished before speaking.

"Mother," Christopher softly called, "Will you talk to me?"

"What do you want?" she called back.

"I just want to talk. I heard you singing and your words filled my heart with loneliness."

"Your companions will soon be singing, *Christopher Stoke*," she answered. "They are drinking their strong beer and soon they will sing. You should sing their songs. They are songs from your land, aren't they?"

"They are not," Christopher replied. "I am not one of them. They think I am but I am just pretending."

She put down the bowl. "All right," she sighed. She got up and unfastened the door. "Come in then."

She lit a lamp and Christopher sat beside her. She looked over at him. "What do you want to talk about?" she asked.

"I was curious about your song," he replied. "Is it a love song?"

"It is a hymn of praise to the Foam of the Sea." She glowered at him.

"I am sorry, mistress," he replied. "My Quechua is not good enough to hear all the words in songs. And when you sang it sounded like a love song."

"Why shouldn't I sing a hymn to the Foam of the Sea as a love song?" she demanded. "The priestesses of my order are wives to the Hidden God."

"Of course you are," Christopher soothed. "I see no impropriety. Perhaps one day you will meet him in person."

"Perhaps," she sighed. "Perhaps I will grow wings, like a white egret, and fly over the ocean to find him. Perhaps I will live by his side, his wife in a foreign land."

"Stranger things have happened," Christopher agreed. "And what would you say to him when you met him?"

She turned away from Christopher and looked at the lamp. He let the silence stretch until she spoke. "I would ask him why he left me alone for so long." He heard her voice choke a little. "The last priestess died ten years ago and I have been alone all that time."

"Mother, perhaps he is lonely too."

"He is a god."

"Don't you think that immortality gets lonely?"

"I wouldn't know, *Stoke*. The priestess came to our village and we danced for them. I was chosen: it was a great honour. They told me what a great honour it was as we walked through the mountains and down to the sea. But when we got here the Spanish had taken everything. The priestesses were gone, kidnapped, and we were all that was left. It seemed that the great honour was a life of work. There is too much work for two people."

"Where is she?"

"She died ten years ago. I told you. I am the last."

"How long ago did you come here?"

"It was the year the Spanish came. Forty years ago."

"The Spanish have wounded the hearts of your people, Mother. Wouldn't they have wounded the heart of your god?"

"I wouldn't know," she snapped. Then she looked at him. "Is that why he no longer answers prayers?"

"It could be. Perhaps he needs his wife to heal his heart, Mother."

"What do you know about being a wife, man?" she scorned.

"You might be surprised," Christopher smiled.

"Anyway, how can a god as great as the Foam of the Sea have just one wife?"

"Perhaps one wife is all he needs."

"Have you been married, *Stoke*?"

"I have. But never to a god."

Now he knew he had her attention. She leaned closer. "How does a wife show her husband that she loves him when they meet in person?"

Christopher told her.

By the evening of the second day they had finished to the priestess' satisfaction. John ordered the crew to their camp, fearing their reaction to whatever ritual she might conduct, but he took Gustavo, Philip, Christopher and Barnabas to bring her the things they had gathered. She took them and wandered off, leaving them alone.

"This reeks of pagan idolatry to me," grumbled John.

"He is right," agreed Philip.

"At least she believes in her gods," replied Gustavo. "The priests from the temples back home do not believe in anything except the power of that witch."

"You don't know that," Christopher admonished. "Perhaps the ones that follow the witch are like that, but I am sure that most of them are sincere in their worship."

"I will never trust them again," said Gustavo. "I would better trust some old brown woman we found in the wilderness."

"Good," interrupted Barnabas, "Because trusting the brown woman is the way to find what we are looking for."

"You would know all about pagan idolatry, though, wouldn't you?" accused John.

"This isn't helping," said Christopher. "Her beliefs cannot do you any harm, but her guidance can take us to what we seek. We should help her. She doesn't need us to participate in her rituals. She says it is forbidden anyway. If you didn't want us to help her with her preparations, though, you should have spoken up days ago."

"Before we spent all that time catching those two birds?" asked John.

"Before I got cut to pieces trying to pick those thorn-berries?" asked Barnabas.

"Before I nearly got bitten by that snake?" asked Philip.

"Before I swept out that courtyard like some servant girl?" asked Gustavo.

"Yes, before all of those things. Before I found her herbs, too. We've done our part. Now let us see what happens. We can talk about it in the morning."

They looked at one another. Philip shrugged. "We will most certainly talk about this in the morning, though," he said.

"Meanwhile, if we can watch without interrupting, let us see what she does. I think it might be quite a show."

Christopher looked from one to the other as they agreed. He knew them well, now, and was alert for signs that they might have second thoughts. They sat down and Christopher sat between John and Barnabas, since they were the biggest risks.

The priestess spent a long time huddled, sat on her heels, as the Sun set behind them and vanished into the ocean. There was nothing much to see from the distance but Christopher knew she was labouring to kindle a new fire. Finally they saw the wisp of smoke curl up. She took the fire over to the heaped wood and fanned the flames. In the dry breeze it soon took hold.

Then she stood up and began to speak. Christopher could hear that she was addressing Mother Earth and Her Son, but of course the rest of them didn't have a word of Quechua between them. She chanted the liturgy as she walked around and defined her ritual space. Christopher noted that their little party of Europeans was outside the boundary.

Then her voice changed. She broke off the chanting and began an impassioned prayer, calling on the Hidden God, the Foam of the Sea, to guide her. She was closing the temple that she had served all her years and going out in the world, with no idea where to go and what to do. She promised to follow his foam-flecked footsteps wherever they took her, but she needed guidance. There was no other priestess to help her or offer her wisdom, just five mad foreigners who knew nothing. It even begged her god to remember that today she had lived fifty years on the Earth.

Then she broke off her personal prayer and went back to the words of the ritual. She stumbled here and there as she tried to remember, but her voice was confident. She spoke to the sky, offering sacrifice, then she released the two birds. They whirred up into the evening sky and flew away to the North, among the first stars. She praised their flight, comparing it to the words of humans rising into–

Christopher realised John was whispering to him. "What did you say?" he whispered back, switching his thoughts from Quechua to English. He could see that John was scared. "What is it?"

John pointed to the North. "There," he said. "Look."

Christopher looked over at the horizon but he could see nothing except the smoke rising from Ciudad de los Reyes. The birds had gone. "What is it?" he asked.

"Cassiopeia," he said.

"Cassiopeia?" Christopher asked.

"It's a constellation," Barnabas answered from behind Christopher. "It's not one of the Zodiac."

Philip looked around from behind John. "Ptolemy named the constellation. Cassiopeia was Queen of Ethiopia. Greek legend says that–"

"Can't you learned fools see what is in front of your face?" interrupted John. "There is an extra star!"

"Which one?"

"Cassiopeia is two triangles touching," said John, "Shaped like the letter W. That star there is new. It is getting brighter, too."

"Is it a planet?" asked Christopher.

"A planet would be over our heads," replied Barnabas. "As I said, Cassiopeia is not in the Zodiac."

"Is it a shooting star?" asked Philip.

"It's not shooting anywhere," muttered John. "Unless it is coming straight for us."

"Well, we said we would talk about it in the morning."

They sat and watched as the priestess completed her rite until finally she took a bucket and threw water in every direction around her perimeter, erasing the boundaries of the ritual space. Then she started to walk towards them. Christopher looked up to the North. The new star was now the brightest thing in the heavens. The old priestess chuckled to herself. She came and spoke to Christopher, then wandered off, still laughing to herself.

"What did she say?" asked Barnabas.

"Anyone can tell," answered Philip. "She is saying that the new star is her god's doing."

John frowned. "So this is some blasphemous Nativity scene, with us in the part of wise men?"

"Some of us are wise," suggested Barnabas. "Others–"

"Well, Doctor Stoke," said Gustavo, watching her go, "You promised us a show." He stared up at the new star. "And you have certainly delivered on that promise."

Christopher shrugged. "It's none of my doing," he replied.

* * *

The last priestess of the Hidden God walked up the path. Steps were cut in the rock and she placed one after another, not hurrying but never letting the pace slacken either. Behind her four European men struggled to keep up. As they climbed the mist drifted past, clouds torn ragged as they were dragged through the jagged mountains. The sound of rain falling hissed around them but behind that sound they could hear a bass rumble, growing with each step.

"Palla," called Christopher, struggling to catch up with her, "*What is that sound?*"

"*That is the Great Speaker,*" she told him. "*You will see soon enough. When we are over this rise and in the next valley you will see.*"

"What did she say?" puffed John.

"She says it is *Apurimac*," answered Christopher.

"What is an Apurimac?" asked Philip.

"It means Great Speaker," said Christopher. "And now you know as much as I do."

"How long are we going to follow her?" asked John. "We could still be doing this come Christmas."

"We're not even half way through December," Christopher said.

"I know you tell us the date but I don't even know how you keep it straight in your head," John grumbled. "Every day seems the same. It is like being at sea without a logbook."

"Well, things are changing. When we started this we were walking through desert. Since we have come into the mountains it has been getting more and more wet."

"This is wet enough," agreed John. "At least in a ship you can go below and try and dry out a little bit."

"Palla keeps finding us these shelters," said Christopher. "And she speaks to locals and they take us in and feed us."

"But only for one night," John replied. "Then first thing in the morning she expects us to be back on the road. How does she do it in this air?"

"Have you seen the leaves she chews?"

"That bush? It is far too bitter."

"It contains an essence that makes it easier to endure high altitudes."

"Well, Doctor Stoke, I am not that desperate yet."

They trudged along without any more speech. Looking up into the driving rain they sought the end of each flight of stairs cut into the rock, but each time they came over a rise they just saw another. The rumbling ahead of them grew to a roar and the mist came thick, blown by a cold, wet wind.

Then they reached their first step down. Now things went quicker as they descended the slippery steps. The mist lightened and then suddenly cleared.

Below them the valley stretched away. It looked like a canyon of rocks covered in thick moss, but they knew from walking these mountains that the moss was great trees covering rocks as big as castles. But the bottom of the valley was filled with furious white water. Everything seemed to move slowly but, as they glimpsed trees tumbling in the chaos, they saw that this was an illusion caused by great distance.

"*The Great Speaker,*" said the priestess. "*I have not seen it since I was a girl.*"

"*How do we cross it, Mother?*" asked Christopher.

"*There is a bridge,*" she replied. "*Or at least there was forty years ago.*"

Christopher relayed this news to the others as they walked down into the valley. From high up the water moved with majestic grace, but closer to it defied the senses. The path followed beside the river and they walked along with that roar battering their heads all afternoon, until their ears sang and their throats were sore with the effort of shouting over it.

In the morning the priestess led them into the new light and along the valley still further. She came around the curve of one mountain and pointed ahead of them. It looked as if someone had strung a rope across the valley. But as they got closer they realised that the sodden cord that swung in the wind was their bridge. The road climbed a short way and they saw that the end of the cord was a ribbon folded lengthwise to make a crude channel.

Barnabas pointed at it and laughed. Christopher did not say anything. Even Philip and Gustavo were reluctant. But the priestess just stepped onto the bridge as if it was a street in any normal town.

"Come on, lads," said John. "It can't be any worse that climbing the rigging on our own *Dragonfly.*"

"Perhaps if we could be sure that this was as strong as honest hemp," replied Philip. "But it looks to me as if it is just grass-blades plaited together."

John stepped onto the swaying bridge. "Look," he said, "It is strong enough."

Barnabas looked down at the roiling water. "Why don't we wait and see if you and the mad woman make it across?" he said.

"I had better not need to come back for you," warned John.

"You won't," answered Gustavo. "I'll get him moving, John."

"But it would be good not to put too much weight on it," said Christopher. "Perhaps you can go ahead."

John held on to the sides of the bridge as he crossed and thought back to his days as a young lad working the top-sails. He kept his eyes focused on the other bank, deliberately ignoring the mass of water roaring beneath his feet. For a second something caught his eye and he looked left. He saw a stick pitching and rolling in the river. As he watched it caught on the bottom and tumbled over, leaping out of the water like a whale breaching. As it sped beneath him he realised the stick was a whole tree, torn away by the flow. A moment later it was gone.

He breathed deeply and looked ahead to the rocky river bank. One foot after another, he told himself. The priestess was talking to a man with a pair of the odd animals that passed for beasts of burden here in this land. Both animals were loaded down with sacks. As he got closer John saw the man make a gesture of deference to their priestess.

"Hello," he said to the man, knowing that he could not understand. The priestess made some comment which he suspected was a joke at his expense and the man smiled.

Christopher was the next one over. He spoke to them both in Quechua. "*I am sorry for the delay,*" he said. "*We are not used to your bridges.*"

The man smiled to himself. "*It is fun to watch,*" he said. "*Better is when the soldiers cross with horses. Your horses are even more nervous than your soldiers. And it gives me more time to talk with the priestess.*"

"*We will have to be going soon,*" the priestess said. "*But the Mother of the Earth will watch over you when we are gone.*"

"*Yes, Mother,*" the man replied. "*Pray for me,* Mamacona."

As soon as Gustavo had hurried Barnabas over the bridge the man took his leave of them and drove his two llamas ahead. The bridge sagged as they walked towards the middle but it held, and it stayed above the water. They were over.

As they walked down the pass the city before them came into view. At first the roofs looked like any Spanish colonial town but, as they got closer, they saw that the city walls were not Spanish. Every stone was different, each one polished and shaped to fit its neighbours. No stone-mason in Europe would buld a wall that way.

But the top of the wall looked very familiar. Above the gate stood soldiers in Spanish armour, carrying pikes and muskets. In front of them, set into the stones of the wall, there were metal poles. The metal poles were surmounted by heads. Barnabas pointed out one head.

"There, that one is the god," he said. "We're wasting our time."

"What is he talking about now?" asked John.

"Things that are way beyond your philosophy, master sailor," sneered Barnabas.

"Christopher, can you ask Palla?" asked Philip.

"I will," said Christopher. "But, while I am doing it, you gentlemen could perhaps figure out how we are going to smuggle four Englishmen into the town." He turned to the priestess. "*Mother*," he began in Quechua, "*Our seer says that one of the heads on the gate belongs to your god.*"

"*I am no seer,*" she replied. "*But let me look.*"

Christopher turned to John. "May we borrow your spy-glass?"

"Don't break it." John handed it over and Christopher extended it and focused it on the city gate. Then, with careful guidance, he helped the priestess to aim it and look through it. "*Oh,*" she said. "*He is the son of the Sun God. Our last king. So it is true, then. The Spanish have defeated us.*"

"She says the head is of their king," Christopher translated.

"The letter said that Toledo had tortured them and that they would not tell him where the golden thing was," said Barnabas.

"That is right," agreed Philip. "Maybe when they were done with him they killed him."

"This is the Inquisition," said Gustavo. "The only way to not answer their questions is to keep silent forever."

"Keep silent forever?" asked John.

"He means the silence of the grave," replied Barnabas. "Dead men don't tell tales."

"Then is there any point in going into the town at all?" asked Philip.

"It is the biggest town for miles around," replied Barnabas. "If there is anything to be found out it will be in there."

"How are we going to get in, then?" asked Christopher.

"The same way we got into Panama," said Gustavo. "I will demand entrance for me and my servants. They will not refuse me: I am the son of knights."

Cuzco

Once they were within the walls of the town they didn't have to walk far. There was a square beside the governor's house. There was a market filled with bustle and, like any square in London or Madrid, the whole was watched by the disembodied heads of criminals, looking down from bloody pikes on the city walls. On another side of the square an old temple had been converted to a cathedral. Gustavo excused himself from the others and slipped inside, into the coolness, to light a candle for the soul of his lost Eva. John made some mutterings about popery but they let it go by.

Inside the cathedral it was cool and dark, out of the Sun, and peaceful. Philip wrinkled his nose at the incense, and both Barnabas Saul and John Overy were uncomfortable with being in a Roman church, for their different reasons, but Gustavo was glad to be there. Gustavo made his way to the Lady Chapel, dropped a coin in the box and lit a candle, then knelt down to pray.

Kneeling there, eyes closed in that familiar space, Gustavo was faced with a new problem. Did he even believe? After all he had seen, could he really pray to God? He opened his eyes again and they fell upon the statue of the Virgin. He saw her turquoise blue cloak and her hair like the golden fleece. Her blue-green eyes stared down at him and he recognised the shape of her face. This Virgin was modelled on the witch who had murdered his Eva! He tried to remember the statue from the church where he had grown up, and then he remembered what Philip had said: if there was a God, surely He would bring the witch to judgement one day. And then, perhaps, Gustavo and his Eva could be together again, for surely gentle Eva could not deserve Hell. But what about Gustavo? Was she to be comforted in the arms of Jesus while he burned in Hell? For Gustavo knew he was an enemy of the Church - but did the Church hold those keys to Heaven that the priests said? This was a rock against which the gates of Hell had surely prevailed. Then what did Jesus' promise to Peter mean?

Instead of prayer, all Gustavo's mind offered was this tide of heresy.

The candle was burning, and he was supposed to be praying for the soul of his poor love. As he worried about his doubts under the gaze of that blasphemous statue, he was interrupted by a touch on the shoulder. He was surrounded by armed men, livery of Don Francisco. They were captured.

Alone in his office Don Francisco found the dagger his mistress had given him. He put his hand on the ancient hilt and thought of her. Suddenly he felt the strange tingle that told him the magic was working.

i hope you have some good news for me

"Yes, Our Lady," he whispered. "I have found the English pirates."

good came the reply. *you are not completely incompetent then*

"I do my best for you, Our Lady."

that is my fear she replied. *so what is the good news*

"They have a priestess with them."

i thought they were all gone

"So did I, Our Lady. But she is really a priestess of the hidden god."

she had better be alive when I get there

"She will be, Our Lady. I promise. She will be alive and willing to tell us everything."

"This is a prison," grumbled Barnabas.

"It is a very well appointed prison," replied Philip.

"All it wants is bars," Barnabas added. He went to the window and opened the shutters. The bright sun of the mountains shone down into the square, three storeys below them. "It would be a long jump," he said.

John leaned out beside him and poked at the walls. "The plaster is too crumbly to offer much of a foothold," he added. He dislodged a piece of it which fell down the wall, tumbling, and smashed on the cobbles below them. A guard looked up, shading his eyes with his hand.

"As I said, all it wants is bars." He looked up to the gate, decorated with the decomposing heads of the last Inka and his family. "You know what the Spanish do to traitors and spies, don't you?"

"Every man has to die, Master Saul," said Philip. "We should make our souls ready to meet our Maker with fortitude and courage."

Christopher could read the doubt in Gustavo's face, and he went over to be near if Gustavo should want to talk. John was watching and Christopher knew he had showed too much emotion in his movements. He was just wondering how to put it right when the doors opened.

It was a servant, dressed in the livery of their captor. Behind him were a dozen guards, waiting in the hallway. The servant bowed. "Gentlemen," he said, "Don Francisco requests your company for dinner."

"Is 'requests' the right word?" Barnabas asked, scornfully.

Gustavo scowled at him. "I am sorry for my companion's ill-humour," he told the servant. "We have had a difficult day. Please tell Don Francisco that we will join him shortly. We are still getting ready after our travels on the road."

The servant bowed and left, and they heard the bar being put on the door.

"Why do we want to dine with some Spanish dog?" asked John.

"Don Francisco is of noble birth," said Gustavo, suddenly aware that they had taken his sword.

"Please, gentlemen," said Christopher. "We should be polite. We should not lower ourselves to his level and, anyway, we should hear what he says. He will think he has us and that it is safe to let his guard down. We might learn something to our advantage."

"He does have us, Doctor Stoke," Philip observed. "Whatever we learn we will take with us to the grave."

"If they even give us a decent burial," suggested Gustavo, looking out at the heads on the city gate.

John looked at Christopher. "Do you have a plan for our escape?"

"Not yet," Christopher replied. "I think the best plan is to simply wait and see if the opportunity presents itself. Meanwhile, we mustn't give up hope."

The servant came back with his guard after a while and the five of them allowed him to lead them down into the hall. Don Francisco was waiting and Christopher could see impatience in the way he stood. He was an older man, dressed in finery that was slightly worn. His beard was trimmed but his face was darkened by the Sun and lined by the mountain wind. He composed his face with a welcoming smile and came over to them. "My house is your house," he said.

"Thank you for your hospitality," Gustavo smiled.

Don Francisco turned to the servants. "Bring wine for our guests," he said, "And tell them in the kitchen that we will dine now."

The servants brought wine in silver goblets. "Let us drink to long life," Don Francisco suggested. He looked at Barnabas as he said it.

"Ay," agreed Philip. "Let us drink to the eternal life that is God's reward for doing His work."

Don Francisco smiled. "Do you still believe in that?" he asked.

"Of course," Philip replied. "Why wouldn't I?"

Don Francisco dismissed the idea with a shrug. "Very well," he said.

The servants brought the food in and, in spite of their situation, they sat down readily enough. Philip sat on one side of Don Francisco and Gustavo sat on the other, with Christopher beside Philip and Barnabas beside Gustavo. Christopher couldn't help but notice that this put the bulk of John as far from Don Francisco as possible.

"Are you enjoying your visit to the New World?" Don Francisco asked.

"It is interesting enough," replied Gustavo.

"We find we have many questions," said Philip.

"Then ask," replied Don Francisco. "I am not a scholar, but perhaps I can offer a few answers."

"The roads do not seem suited to horses and carriages," observed Philip. "How do you move men around?"

"The savages of this country had no knowledge of the wheel, or the horse," replied Don Francisco. "The roads need improvement but they are sufficient for now. Perhaps in places a company of men are compelled to go in single file and lead their horses, but this is mountain country."

"These roads are hardly made for knights," said Gustavo.

"I don't have knights, Don Gustavo," Don Francisco replied. "I have king's men and I have mercenaries, an army of mixed natives and Spaniards. We have no need of knights."

"Besides," suggested Gustavo, "the chivalric code of knights would get in the way of what you do here."

"Your friend Philip believes in God and you believe in chivalry. What old-fashioned philosophies your company has."

Gustavo stood up, his hand straying to the hilt of the sword he no longer possessed. "Some of us come from ancient lines of knights. The code of the knight is what the kingdom of Spain stands upon.

"Not any more," smiled Don Francisco. "The only use the king has for knights is to pay his taxes. Soon they will be so impoverished that they will be nothing but old men to be laughed at for clinging on to old ideas that have passed their time. And, when they die, chivalry will be gone from the world. There will be nothing but the word of the king and the word of the Church – and both will rule according to the will of my mistress."

"So then, as we are speaking of old, tell us about your mistress," Christopher suggested, before Gustavo could continue.

Don Francisco's smile became broader. "Do you know what she is?" he asked.

"I know far better than you do," Christopher replied. "I know that the day you cease to be useful to her, she will dispose of you."

"Then I will have to continue to be useful to her." He looked at the sneer on Christopher's face and added, "Do you know what we are searching for, here in this mountain kingdom?"

"*El Dorado,*" said Christopher. "The golden prize."

"You Spanish only care about gold," accused Philip.

"And what is it that brings the English pirates to these shores, do you think?" Don Francisco looked straight at Philip. "Master Sidney, it is gold that brings ignorant men to these shores, be they from France, Holland, Spain, Portugal or England. All pirates are driven by the same greed. But the thing we seek is far greater than mere gold. Our Lady is a magician of an ancient order, from the days when magic ruled the Earth. When Atlantis fell magic was locked away, beyond the reach of all but the oldest. The thing we seek is the key to unlock it."

"And what then?" asked Christopher.

"Then she will use her magic to conquer the world," Don Francisco replied. He glanced over at Barnabas. "And then, when the whole world is hers, she will reward her loyal followers."

The man opened a door and peered into the gloom. He was bulky and dark: he had been a soldier before the Spanish came.

"Mamacona," he said in Quechua, "Your presence honours this house."

The old woman hardly stirred: in the darkness it was only the clink of the chains that showed that she had moved at all. The man crouched beside her and raised her chin. "I know who you are and so do they," he whispered. "You will tell them everything, Mamacona."

She opened her eyes and glared at him. "You have forgotten who I serve," she told him.

"The Inka is dead."

"I never served the Inka," she smiled. "I serve the Hidden God. He will save me. When your masters have destroyed you I will live in his mansion for the rest of my days."

He laughed as he reached for his tools. "You will be singing a different song soon, Mamacona."

* * *

Jane Fisher's Diary,
Cuzco,
Saturday 20 December 1572 (Julian Calendar).

Tomorrow it will be seven months since we sailed from England. We are guests of the Governor of Cuzco. Although the rooms we have been given are quite luxurious by Sixteenth Century standards, they might as well be dungeons. We are prisoners here and, if we do not escape, we will soon be guests of Eva de Castilla. She reminded me over and over that it would be a disaster, a threat to my existence and that of everyone and everything I have known, if I were to fall into her hands. So we must escape.

I can't help remembering what they taught me in college. When I was an undergraduate my lecturer used to emphasise, again and again, how our profession means compassion for everyone. Later when I became a lecturer I taught it to students myself. I even remember Catherine Howard coming to the department and talking about it. Compassion, always compassion. But we lived in such a rarefied culture, where we never had to face true evil. Now I am facing the reality of human history and the words of professors no longer seem relevant.

As we rode into Cuzco we saw the heads on spikes that stare out over the walls. In a society with no way of discovering and intercepting crimes, those heads offer a deterrent of sorts to those that would betray the king and his representative. But we asked around. Some of the heads on spikes are those of the true king of this land and his household. They tortured him to death, but first they tortured his wives and sons before his eyes. He watched everyone he loved killed, the hopes of his house destroyed, because he would not give away some secret. The man who allowed this to happen, who ordered women and children brutalised for his mistress, is our charming host Francisco de Toledo.

I read about this sort of thing in history. I was conceited enough to consider myself an expert in history, and the people around me were ignorant enough to believe it. I published papers, telling everyone how the compassion of one of us would have transformed those societies I studied. But, when faced with the reality of what was once in books, I find that I don't want to help him to be a better person. I find I want his head on a pole beside his victims. I know I should be thinking of how his outer violence is a reflection of his inner conflicts, and how I should be trying to offer him healing as even-handledly as I should be offering healing to his victims. I know we are supposed to be healers, not judges. But I just want him dead. How can I do anything else but judge when faced with such evil?

I guess I am not Catherine Howard after all. Or perhaps, were she transported to this savage land, maybe she would become as savage as this land herself: as savage as I am becoming.

Sweet Jesus, I need to go home.

The door was un-bolted and opened. Servants brought lamps in for them. They were about to go when Christopher spoke up. "Wait," he said. "Surely you don't expect us to get ourselves to bed?" He looked at Gustavo. "Don Gustavo?" he asked.

"It is true," said Don Gustavo. "I want my bed made and warmed."

The servants looked at the guards and the guard's leader shrugged. The servants were left with them and the doors closed and bolted once more.

Christopher wasted no time. "*Gentlemen,*" he said in his best Quechua, hoping he had the honorific right, "*can you tell us any news of our travelling companion?*"

"*The Mother?*" one of them asked, wide-eyed.

"*She is the last priestess of the Foam of the Sea.*" Christopher explained.

"*Then that is why the foreigners are torturing her,*" replied the servant. "*They are searching for him.*"

"*How do you know?*"

"*I was a courtier to the King before the strangers killed the royal family. They demanded the same question. They are searching for our gods. I do not know why.*"

"*Don Francisco told us why. They have a goddess of their own. She wants to steal something from your gods. It is very important that she doesn't get it.*"

"*Do you think his last priestess would betray him to the Spanish? We are made of sterner stuff than that. They will torture her but she will tell them nothing.*"

"*Their goddess is coming here.*"

"*Do you think she is as powerful as our gods?*"

"*I don't know. I think she is more powerful than one of his priestesses.*"

"*Then what can we do?*"

"*Help us escape.*"

"*How? The guards are foreigners. They will not help us.*"

"What are they saying?" asked Barnabas. "They're telling you that they won't help, aren't they?"

"They are worried about the guards," Christopher replied.

"I can deal with the guards," said Barnabas. "I will give them some berries they can feed to the guards."

"Berries?" asked Christopher. "Is this to make them sleep?"

"Yes, it will make them sleep for a long time," agreed Barnabas with a grin. "The berries do not have a strong flavour and only a little is needed."

Christopher turned back to the servant and switched to Quechua. "*If you give them a herb to make them sleep, you will not need to worry about them.*"

"*Where will we find such a thing?*"

"*I am a physician,*" Christopher replied. "*I will provide you with what you need.*"

Christopher watched as the old servant made up his mind. "*Very well,*" he said. "*I will help you.*"

Christopher Stoke was dreaming when someone shook his shoulder. As he sat up Christopher saw and smelled a man leaning over him in the darkness. He woke up just fast enough to suppress his scream.

"*Wake up! Wake up!*" the man was saying in Quechua. "*Your 'sleeping herb' has worked on them.*"

Christopher sat up. "*Show me,*" he said.

The man led him out past the door. The guards were lying on the floor, twisted into unnatural positions, vomit and foam on their noses and mouths. Neither was breathing. *Sleeping herb,* Christopher thought guiltily. "*I will wake the others,*" he said. "*I need to find the priestess and our equipment.*"

"*I know where the priestess is,*" said the servant. "*They have been torturing her.*"

"I knew it," Christopher muttered to himself. "*I will come with you when I have woken the others. We will need our equipment if we are to travel.*"

"*Where will you go?*"

"*We need to find the god. Where should we look?*"

"*Go along the royal road north and west of here,*" the servant replied. "*Go to the City of the Ancient Peak. The priestess will know the way.*"

"*Can you find* horses?" asked Christopher.

"*What are* horses?" asked the servant. "*Oh, you mean* caballos? *I will find some for you.*" He hurried off.

Christopher woke the others just as the servants returned. "Sleeping draught?" he asked Barnabas.

"They deserved it," Barnabas muttered.

"They surely did," agreed Philip. "But it is too late to argue anyway. The deed is done. Let us get moving, Doctor Stoke."

"I need to find the priestess." They looked at each other, but nobody argued. "The servants are finding horses," Christopher added. "Get them packed. We need to escape quickly and quietly."

The servants led Christopher to the cell where they held the priestess. "Palla," he called, "*Mother, are you hurt?*"

"*Just my fingers,*" she replied. "*I can walk.*"

He took her hands. The fingers were crushed and crooked. "*I'm going to straighten them and then I am going to bind them up. It will hurt, I am afraid.*"

"*Of course it will hurt,*" she answered, giving him her hands. "*Do you think I am a child?*"

She endured silently while he set the bones and joints as best he could and bound them together. Then he led her out to where the horses waited. "*I won't be able to hold on,*" she said.

"What is she saying?" asked John.

"She says she cannot ride," Christopher replied. "John, can you set her before you?"

"I can, but we will need to take an extra horse. This one will tire quickly if it is carrying two."

They rode out of the stables and out on to the street. The night was dark and the city silent until they got to the gates. Guards jumped to attention.

"*Let me through!*" shouted Gustavo. "I have a long way to ride today."

"Yes, sir!" they replied, as they un-barred the gates.

They rode out onto the north-west road. Once they had climbed out of the valley and were out of sight of the city, Philip called a halt. "Where are we going?" he asked.

"The City of the Ancient Peak," Christopher answered.

They did not reach any city that evening. Instead the priestess found them another roadside campground and they bedded down. They were high in the mountains, well out of reach of the Spanish, and all tired from the night of their escape and a long day of riding. They set watches but none of them believed it was necessary. What happened next was perhaps inevitable.

Barnabas was awoken by the sharp thing prodding at his ribs. "What do you want?" he shouted, sitting up. "Get those things away from me!" He looked around where the others slept. "Doctor Stoke," he shouted, "Wake up and tell these fellows not to point their spears at me."

Christopher took a moment to wake up and realise that he was the doctor that Barnabas was addressing. He sat up and realised he, too, was surrounded by spears. *"Good evening,"* he began in Quechua, *"I would like to..."* He saw the reactions of them and realised that they did not understand him.

Then the priestess spoke. Christopher could not follow what she said but he saw the spear-points waver. As she berated them for their disrespect they hung their heads.

As she slowed down he tried to interrupt. "Mamacona," he began, *"Who are these people?"*

"They are mountain folk," she said, *"But they should know better than to attack the entourage of a priestess."*

"Of course," agreed Christopher. *"Now what happens?"*

"They say that they know where the old Inka's guard lives," the priestess smiled. *"Now they take us to the City of the Ancient Peak."*

It had been a hard climb for a woman who had lived more than fifty years, but with every step her aching legs took her she felt herself entering a world where she belonged. The Spanish invaders had occupied the valleys but her people still lived in the mountains. And among her people she was someone of note: the high priestess; the last priestess. She saw how they looked at her and whispered, and she felt self-conscious. But it was a good kind of self-consciousness, mingled as it was with pride. It was her reward for forty years of faithfulness.

They let her cross the bridge and enter the City of the Ancient Peak, the summer palace of the Son of the Sun. She could see ahead of her the division in the city, how the lower part had meaner houses and terraces, but the palaces and courtyards of the upper city beyond it. Her companions were led away and she was about to follow them, but one of the guards spoke. "Come with us, Mama," he said. "You don't belong with these foreigners."

She looked back at them. Christopher spoke. "Go on, Mother," he said. "We are strangers but you belong here. You are the last priestess of the Foam of the Sea, after all."

The priestess allowed them to lead her away, through the narrow gate and into the upper city. "That stranger speaks our language," remarked one of the guards. "I have never seen one of the strangers speak our language."

"Neither had I," she replied. "But I have not known many strangers."

"The strangers never speak our language, Mother," the other guard replied. "They expect us to learn theirs."

They crossed the courtyard together and went into the palace. The guard at the door stopped her. "Who is this?" he asked, looking at her worn clothing and lined face.

"This is the High Priestess of the Temple of Pachacamac," one of her guards replied. "She has walked all the way from the coast and escaped a Spanish prison to be here tonight." He smiled. "I think He should be told that she is here, don't you think?"

"Perhaps. But He is resting. I don't want to disturb Him."

"Tell Him that His wife is here."

The priestess turned to the guard beside her. "I am nobody's wife," she objected. "I am the last priestess."

"But you are someone's wife, Mother," the guard replied. "You are wife to the Foam of the Sea."

"That is right," the guard at the door said. "Very well. I will tell Him that you are here." He hurried off and the other two led her into the outer room. They ordered the servants to find her food.

She was sitting and eating the warm meal when the door opened. The guards and the servants all jumped to their feet, but she had no idea who she was looking at. The man at the door was bent with age, but his sagging shoulders were still higher than her head. He came over to her and sat beside her. The chair creaked as it took his weight. He put his hand on hers. She glanced down at it. The skin of his hand was so old and white it made her seem a little girl by comparison. She looked up at his face and suddenly she knew.

"Oh," she said. "You are..." She put down her spoon and slid off her chair to kneel at his feet. In her mind she tried to remember the words, the liturgy, but the old priestess who trained her had never taught her how to address her god when she met him in person.

$$— 10 —$$

The Hidden God

The guards led them to a small thatched cottage and opened it for them. *"In here,"* the guard said in Quechua as he pointed. *"Bring food."* He pointed at his open mouth, then made a show of closing his eyes and lowering his head. *"Then sleep,"* he added.

"Thank you," replied Christopher. *"Will the priestess be taken care of?"*

The guard blinked, then looked a little embarrassed. *"I am sorry,"* he said. *"I was told that you foreigners couldn't speak our language."*

"It is only me who can," agreed Christopher. *"But I will tell my companions."*

"Well, I will find food," the guard said. He excused himself.

"You surprised him," said Philip. "Where did you learn their language, Doctor Stoke?"

"That is too long a story for tonight," apologised Christopher. "May we leave it for some other time?"

Barnabas found a lamp and whispered a few words to summon a fire elemental. A moment later the brightness glimmered on the walls and in the roof. The door opened again: the guard had returned with food. It was a sort of yellow porridge enlivened with pieces of meat and some sort of green and red vegetables. It was perhaps a little spicy for the tastes of Philip, John and Barnabas, but they were too tired to care.

The guard saw them start to eat, then saw their lamp flicker. *"The wind is getting in!"* he exclaimed. *"We mustn't have you catching colds. What would happen if the priests came to bring you into his presence and you were all dead of cold?"* He bustled around making sure the shutters were carefully sealed.

Only when they were closed to his satisfaction did he leave them.

* * *

The priestess followed him as he walked back to his chambers. The look from the guards showed that they were forbidden to follow, but she was not a guard. She was the last priestess. When he got to his room he turned and stood before her, his hand on the door. "Give me your hands," he said.

She put her hands in his, trustingly. He looked at how her fingers were bound together. "Who hurt you?" he asked.

"The Spanish," she said. "They are looking for you."

"Did you tell them about this place?"

"Of course not," she objected. "What do you think I am?"

"I think you are the last priestess," he said. "Your faithfulness impresses me, even if I don't deserve it." He began to unwrap the bindings on her hands. She kept her face stoic: only the tiniest tensions around her mouth and eyes gave her pain away. Then he took her fingers in his and whispered words. She had never heard such words and they distracted her more than the pain did. As he spoke, he pulled her fingers straight again. "There," he said. He let go.

She flexed her fingers, exploring them, feeling for the pain and finding none. "Thank you, lord," she breathed.

"The servants will find somewhere for you to sleep," he said.

"My lord," she replied, "I am your wife."

"I don't even know your name."

"I am Waqar, my lord."

He stopped speaking and looked at her. "Who gave you that name?" he asked at last.

"My mother, of course." She smiled at him. "Do you like it? I haven't used it since the old priestess died. Perhaps you would prefer something else?"

"One of the things about living so long is that after a while everything reminds you of something or someone. Keep the name your mother gave you." He remembered why she was there. "The priestesses were always told that they were my wives, but how many wives does one man need? If I let priestesses share my bed there would be no room for me. Nor would there be enough peace for me to sleep. Jealousy is not a restful emotion."

"Perhaps when I was a girl that was true, my lord. The old priestess told me there were hundreds. But when we got back to the temple, they were all gone. The Spanish had taken all of them. That was forty years ago."

"I know."

"So you see, my lord, you have just one wife now. There is no jealousy. And if there is no space for me in your bed, my lord, I will sleep on the floor."

He sighed and stepped back to allow her in. She closed the door behind her. He turned away and began to undress, ignoring her. She saw how his hands trembled and she went over and began to help him.

"Waqar, what are you doing?" he asked, looking down at her hands on his body.

"You are my husband, my lord," she told him. She looked up into his face for the first time since she had realised who and what he was. He saw her eyes shining in the darkness.

"I am an old man."

"Sometimes a young woman marries an old man, my lord. They say she can give her youthfulness to him, give him more years of life."

"I think I am a little beyond that. A young woman who marries an old man ought to find herself a discreet lover."

"She should try with her husband first, my lord."

He sighed again. "Have you ever..?"

"Never, my lord," she replied. "I am a priestess."

"If you have romantic ideas they will end in disappointment, you know."

"I'm not ignorant, my lord. But the years in your service have been lonely."

"Very well," he agreed. "You can sleep here. But I cannot promise anything more than that."

The old man woke up. He could not sleep with the sounds of the wind outside. Beside him the priestess quietly snored and around him the mountain wind sighed through the thatch and rattled the shutters. He muttered to himself then, as his eyes adapted to see by the starlight shining around the shutters and the door-frame, he got up and found his clothes. He wrapped himself up carefully against the cold outside and opened the door.

As he walked down to the lower part of the town the guards stiffened. They stood trying to look alert as he shuffled past them. He kept his hands on the walls and looked carefully at the steps illuminated in the starlight. The starlight cast sharp shadows which made it hard for his hazed-over eyes to identify the edges of them. He did not want to slip on the stone steps. His bones were fragile. He knew that he would only have to nurse them through a few more years before they could be discarded. He refused to think about what would happen then.

The town guard had put the barbarians in a house near the square, where the town would meet to discuss their fate. The old man made his way down. He wasn't particularly looking for them but he had an idea that he could maybe look at their equipment or their horses to try and gauge something about where they were from. Perhaps they were part of the Spanish invasion or perhaps they were something else.

One of them was standing in the square, looking up at the new star. The old man watched as the barbarian wandered a little then sat and looked from the mountaintop back up to the star. He thought he would speak to her and see if she would offer any clues. He shuffled up behind her and she jumped. Her noise of surprise was deeper than he expected.

The barbarian turned and the old man saw the young face in profile. He realised his eyes were missing details: the barbarian had a moustache and the beginnings of a young beard. For all that he had seemed to move like a woman the barbarian was male.

Before he could remember words to communicate in their language the barbarian spoke. "Sit down, my lord." The old man drew breath as he recognised the language he had learned from his mother.

"Do you know who I am?" the old man asked.

"I do," the barbarian replied. "But my companions do not and I am not going to tell them. My name is *Chris Stoke* and I am the healer for our company."

The old man sat beside Doctor Stoke. "And will you tell me how you know that language?" he asked.

"I won't," Doctor Stoke replied. "I will apologise for my accent, though. Although I learned it at University, I don't believe my teacher ever heard it spoken by a native."

"Then you have done remarkably well to be understood at all," the old man replied. "And I thank you. I never expected to hear it spoken again."

"You will, though. Don't you realise that the woman who is leader of your enemies speaks the same language?"

"I never realised that my enemies were led by a woman. I am told the enemy leader is a man called *Francisco de Toledo*."

"*Francisco de Toledo* is her servant. She is searching for something."

"So she is. And what do you know about that, *Chris Stoke?*"

"I know that I am here to help you keep it from her."

"Look at me," the old man replied. "Don't you think, perhaps, that you are a few years too late?"

"Immortality doesn't mean living forever, my lord, but you can live a good few years yet."

"My Immortal Breath has failed. In truth I am surprised I have lasted as long as I did." He looked at Stoke with watery blue eyes. "Do you know how old I am?"

"You have six thousand nine hundred and forty-eight summers, my lord. You are the oldest human alive."

"Our Immortal Breath fails eventually. I have seen it before. We had a woman who knew the secret of reversing the process but she is long dead. Do you know how she died, *Christopher Stoke?*"

"You can tell me if you wish, my lord. Or you can ask me the age of the woman who rules the Spanish."

"I see," the old man replied. "Very well," he said disinterestedly, "How old is the woman who rules the Spanish?"

"She has six thousand five hundred and sixty-seven winters, my lord."

Stoke watched as the old man calculated the numbers in his head. "I see," he said. "But why should I care?"

"Because she is young and her 'Immortal Breath' seems to be fine. Do you think she is stronger than you?"

"I think she might be. Her mind was split and one of her personalities was certainly higher Rank than me."

Stoke looked confused and the old man watched his face carefully and wondered why the information had such a strong effect. "There is something else," Stoke said at last.

"I am weary, *Christopher Stoke,* more weary than you can possibly imagine. I need to sleep. It is time you left me in peace."

"Very well, my lord. But think about what I have said, if it pleases you."

"Go on," the old man chided.

Stoke went.

The old man shuffled back through the palace, quietly, trying not to disturb the servants. He was trying to understand. He was suspicious of the woman who was now confirmed to be his enemy and that strange woman-in-man that called him/herself *Christopher* was just further confirmation of his fears. After so many years had passed he had concluded he must be the last. But he had been wrong. He had been complacent and she had built up her power somewhere across the sea. Meanwhile his own power had dwindled away. *Christopher* was right. He had lost his Breath. He remembered the last days of the City and his own mistakes, the opportunities he had thrown away.

He had already closed the door in his own room when he remembered that he was not alone. There was that priestess who had insisted on staying by his side. He sat on his bed.

"My lord," she whispered.

"Don't call me that," he whispered back. "I am nobody's lord."

"When they came to my village to choose us, they said they were seeking brides for you."

"I am sorry about that, Waqar. It wasn't what I wanted them to do."

"Then who did?"

"People do things to remind themselves of society's structure. Society's rules are only in their imaginations, but human imagination is what governs our lives."

"I don't understand, my lord."

"Of course you don't."

There was a silence and he lay down on his bed. He thought she might have gone to sleep but she spoke again. "My lord?" she asked.

"What do you want?"

"If you don't want me to call you that, what do you want me to call you? I told you my name, my lord."

"The name I had when I was a child no longer fits me." He sighed that deep breath she had noticed was his habit. "If you want to call me something, call me Atok. I lived on the edge of civilisation and then I led the pack that tore it to pieces."

"Were you really that bad?"

"I was."

"Then I will call you Atok. It hardly fits with the Kon Tiki I thought I served, though."

"I didn't ask you to serve me at all." As soon as he had said it he realised what those words must mean to her. "Waqar, I know you have devoted your life to an idea. I played my own part in that idea too."

"What about the legends, my lord? They told me that you have mastery over the elements."

"I did when I was younger, even a hundred years ago. My age has crept up on me, like a jaguar stalking its prey. But now I am in its claws."

"Can't I offer you any of my youthfulness? If I am not young enough I can find a girl to be a new priestess."

"It is too late for that." He reached out and touched her skin in the darkness. "The way we live without ageing is to do with the way we breathe. If we allow our minds and emotions to flag we can lose the ability to breathe Immortality. I have gone too far. I will die soon."

"Is there nothing to live for, my lord? What about the Spanish? Couldn't you fight them off?"

"The Spanish are led by one of us. They have a goddess of their own, but one at the height of her power. I thought I was the last."

"Like me?"

"Like you. I thought the ways of us Sea People would die with me. That would be a good thing, Waqar: we were evil. The evil of the Spanish is taught to them by her, but what she is teaching is just an echo of the evil of the City. That evil sent her insane. We were all maimed by it, our hearts imprisoned by hate and fear pretending to be love."

"Maybe we can learn about love together, my lord."

"Waqar, someone tried to teach me about love before."

"What was she like?"

"She was one of us but she was not one of us. She was so young and she had such a great heart. Maybe she had the greatest heart ever."

"Was she like me?"

"She was nothing like you, Waqar. She was named for a white bird too, but not the same kind of bird. She was one of us, one of the Sea People. It took her many years to come into her power but she was always destined to end up... how she ended up."

"She was the one you loved?"

"I loved her, but she wasn't the one I loved. They are all dead now, anyway."

"What happened to her?"

"She died. I... I had to... her love broke the laws of the City and she paid the price."

"Is that why you are afraid to teach me love, my lord?"

"I don't think–"

"You said we should try, my lord."

"I didn't mean..." he stopped, then laughed. "All right. But I think you will be disappointed."

"You already told me that, my lord."

"So I did."

They heard someone at the door. Philip and Gustavo got up and opened it. Two warriors stood there with an older priest in bright clothes.

"What do you want?" Gustavo asked.

The old priest looked at Gustavo with defiance. Christopher squeezed between Gustavo and Philip. "*I apologise for my companions,*" he said in Quechua. "*How can we help you?*"

The priest smiled. "*The City of the Ancient Peak is having a gathering. You are invited.*"

Christopher wasn't sure if the invitation was optional. "Come on," he said to his companions. "We will get to put our case to these people."

"We are being judged by these heathens?" asked John.

"I hope not judged," smiled Christopher. "But if they can help us to find what we seek, then we could benefit from asking nicely."

"Or we could take it from them," suggested Barnabas. "They are ignorant savages. It is probably laying around in some treasure store somewhere. We just need to find it and take it."

"Barnabas Saul," admonished Christopher, "Even if you are not wise enough to recognise the danger of equating lack of English with lack of brains, you should consider that it would be foolish to fight for something that might be given freely."

"Doctor, nobody who truly understands what it is we are seeking would give it up freely. With a hand upon the thing we are seeking, Doctor, a man would become like God Himself. It confers immortality but also the ability to alter any part of the world. We are not talking about the magicians tricks; illusions of one sort or another, flying, finding treasure. We are talking about the ability to destroy or remake the whole world in an instant. With this in my hand I could stand upon creation as my footstool–"

"I think that is enough blasphemy for one morning, Master Saul," growled John.

Barnabas reddened a little but he did not say another word.

Christopher looked at the old priest. "*Take us where we need to go,*" he said.

They were led up steps and into a crowded courtyard. At the opposite end of the courtyard a canopy had been put up. Guards stood around bearing spears and, within their ranks, the priests stood around a throne. There was a stir among them and an old man in a blue blanket shuffled through. He was being supported by a priestess with long, iron-grey hair in a plait. Beneath her headdress they recognised her: it was their own Palla.

The old man was stooped but he was taller than any of them. His hair was white, his skin was pale and his eyes were blue. Palla led him to the throne and he sat down. She sat by his feet. He looked over at them then spoke quietly to one of the priests beside him.

The priest stood straight. *"Bring the visitors forward,"* he commanded in Quechua.

The guards around them encouraged them forward until they stood before the old man on his throne. He looked at each of them in turn. Then he spoke the sort of words that are whispered in that strange place between waking and nightmares. They heard the crowd gasp as silvery light settled around the heads of everyone in the crowd.

"Beware, all of you," whispered Barnabas Saul, "This magic has the power to uncover lies. Keep silent if you do not wish to tell the truth."

"I wish to tell the truth," replied Gustavo.

But the old man interrupted Barnabas' reply. *"Who are you all, and where do you all come from?"* he demanded.

Gustavo was first to speak. *"I come from Spain,"* he replied in Spanish. *"A witch stole my betrothed and I have come here to seek my revenge."*

Philip looked at him, frowning. "We come from England," he said in English. "The woman is opposed to our country and we are looking for a way to thwart her plans."

"How do you people expect to thwart her plans?"

"She has come to this land seeking something," Philip replied. "We do not know what it is but we want to get it before she can."

"And none of you know what it is?"

"I know," Barnabas Saul replied. The rest of them looked at him.

"Do you know where it is?" the old man asked Barnabas.

"I don't," Barnabas said. "But it wouldn't surprise me if you have it."

"It wouldn't surprise me either," the old man replied. The silvery light around his head remained clear and bright.

Barnabas smiled. "May I see it?"

"Not at present," the man answered. *"It is sufficient that you know where it is."* He looked at them. *"Before I pass judgement, do any of you have any reason why I should get involved in your fight?"*

Gustavo replied. "This woman we oppose is evil. Her government is through both the king and the church, and she dominates Europe. She–"

"What is Europe?" asked the old man.

"It is the land where we come from."

"Come closer," the old man said. He took his stick and scratched shapes in the dirt.

Christopher recognised the outlines of all seven continents. "Europe is here," he said. "England is part of an island here. Gustavo comes from Spain, which is here."

John Overy just stared at the map, as if he could memorise it.

Gustavo indicated Christendom with a sweep of his toe. "This area lies under her dominion. She pretends that the people that oppose her are evil, that they oppose God."

"*What is* God?" the old man asked.

For a moment there was silence, then all five of them spoke at once. "*One at a time*," warned the old man. "*My hearing is not what it used to be.*"

"You are being mischievous, my lord," said Christopher Stoke.

"*Perhaps I am. But it is easy for ordinary people to conclude that their rulers are kind or cruel. Ordinary people don't see the complexities of the task. Sometimes a ruler must do things that, were he an ordinary person, he would consider cruel. But from the perspective of the ruler, those things are necessary.*"

"How was it necessary to kill my betrothed?" demanded Gustavo. "She never did anyone any harm. She was killed merely because she happened to resemble that witch."

"She killed her to take her identity," Christopher explained.

"*Then she is not open about her rule?*" asked the old man.

"She is not," agreed Christopher.

"Why are you trying to defend her?" asked Philip.

"*Because she and I are the same. We are both from the same order. If you all knew as much about my rule as you all know about hers, I am sure you all would consider me as cruel as you consider her.*" He laughed a moment. "*If you all knew more, you all would consider me far more cruel. She has killed a few people. I destroyed a civilisation more sophisticated than any on the Earth today.*"

"Then we have come to the wrong place," shrugged Philip. "There is nothing more to be said."

"I think there is more to be said," argued Christopher. "Gustavo, tell him about Madimi."

"Who is Madimi?" asked John.

"Madimi is an angel," said Barnabas.

"Madimi is not an angel," said Gustavo. "She looks like an angel but she is as human as we are. In the same way that Moors are dark and English are fair, Madimi's people are winged. She told me again and again that she was as ordinary as you or me. She is a simple Christian woman, a mother and a widow, who happens to have wings."

"There is a glamour about her that enables her to come and go at will, with none the wiser," said Barnabas.

"*That is written in her blood and her body,*" said the old man. "*Your friend is right: she is as human as any of us. Is she among you people now?*"

"She stayed back in England," said Philip.

"It wouldn't have been safe for her to fall into the hands of the Spanish," added Gustavo. "The Inquisition are seeking her people. They killed her husband and her children. They burned them alive."

"*Why?*" demanded the old man.

"I am sure that from the perspective of a ruler there was a good reason," remarked Gustavo.

Christopher reached into his bag and produced the diary. He opened it at a page he had bookmarked. He stumbled a little over the consonants of the old Atlantean. "*Twenty-Seventh Day of Life, Year of the City 7187. As we suspected the forest is thick with them. This close to Midsummer Day they cannot bear to hide. Rounded up over a hundred of them, mostly females of course.*

"*Fifteenth Day of Midsummer, Year of the City 7187. Following their attempt to break their wives out the final head count was 112 females, 87 males and 94 children. Put them all to the fire. Whatever cold grave you lie in, Aclaí, I wish you could see how...*"

"*That's enough!*" said the old man.

"There is more," said Christopher.

"*I am sure there is,*" he agreed. "*But you have made your point, Christopher Stoke.*"

"Why is she so cruel?" asked Gustavo.

"*Why?*" Muscles in the old man's face flexed as he frowned. "*Never mind why: she is one of the Sea People. We are a savage people from a savage time.*"

"Do our reasons convince you yet?" asked Philip.

"*It turns out that they may persuade me to care. But it doesn't give me the power to do something about it.*" He looked at the guards. "*Take them away again,*" he said. "*I need to think.*"

Waqar followed him into the room. "What is the matter, my lord?" she asked. "Is something the matter, my... Atok?"

"It's that *Christopher Stoke.* He is trying to manipulate me."

"What did he tell you?"

"He told me that... it's a long story."

"I have time," she smiled. She sat down and looked up at him, her eyes eager like a child's. "So, my husband, begin your story."

"This was a long time ago, six thousand years and more. At the time I had a woman who was trying to be my wife, but she was one of us and we are not suited to marriage. Anyway, she wanted to mark the anniversary of my birth. She made me a gift. Well, three gifts, actually: three little servant girls. Let me show you."

He whispered something under his breath. Waqar listened carefully, not wanting to miss anything he said, and then her mind recoiled from what she overheard. She did not understand his words but she knew there was something wrong about them.

But before she could ask him there stood three girls in the room with them. The children had wings that were shaped like those of a moth. Looking closer she could see that their wings were actually made of skin and bone like those of a bat. She also saw that the girls were not really children: the skinny bodies inside their clothes did have the slight outline of breasts. One had yellow hair, one had hair of a pale orange, and one had hair as black as hers had once been framing a pale face with fierce blue eyes. All three of them had the tops of their ears jutting in points though their hair.

"What are they?" she asked.

"They were servants. She was called Day, she was called Twilight and she was called Night."

"Like their hair?"

"That is right. Waqar, I told you that I never had children. That is not true. I put babies in these three. I made sure their babies were like them, and that their blood was pure, but they are my children. When I last saw them there were nearly a hundred of them. Now there must be hundreds of thousands."

"These are the creatures he was describing? Who is trying to kill them?"

"He said it is the woman who created them for me."

"Why would she do that? Did they displease her?"

"I don't know. I never put a baby in her. It was... well, it was sort of forbidden."

"Sort of, my... Atok?"

"My parents were Sea People, just like I was. They brought me to be chosen. But they had to leave our Order when I was on the way. My mother had no choice, of course, but my father had to chose between immortality and the City he loved, or the mother of his child. He chose her and me."

"Of course he did," Waqar replied. "A father has duties."

He looked at her face a moment. "And you think I am neglecting my duties by allowing her to kill them?"

"You are a god, my Atok. I have no right to judge what you do."

"I see." He smiled a rueful smile. "You understand that she is at the height of her power and that I am almost dead?"

"I do realise it." Waqar took her lower lip between her teeth. "I don't want to lose you so soon after I found you. But I will not live much longer than you do. I am fifty years old. I would rather my husband is a dutiful grandparent, though, even if you die in your duty." She reached up and placed a hand on his knee. "Best of all is that you did your duty and came home to me after, though."

He put his hand on hers. "I will try, then. I can limit the power of others but I daren't limit the power of our own Order. When I am dead it might be that my enemy is the only person protecting our world from what is outside. I daren't limit her powers. But I will try and save my grandchildren from her anyway."

Going Forth by Night

Waqar led her newly-found husband up the steps. With one hand he used a stick, with the other arm he leaned on her to steady him. She looked back down along the staircase to the city. They were climbing up the ancient peak itself, the one that gave the city its name. Far below them a great river curved around the peak, filling the valley with thunder.

He stopped to catch his breath, leaning on his stick.

"Where are we going, my Atok?" she asked.

He breathed hard. "The city," he gasped. "I need to save it," he explained. "From her."

"I don't understand," she answered.

He sat on the steps. "We are high enough," he said.

She waited patiently while his breathing subsided. Then he reached up and she helped him to his feet again. He frowned as he tried to remember.

Then he shook his arm to free it from her and climbed two more steps up the staircase. "You might want to sit down, Waqar," he told her.

He turned and stretched out his arms, to encompass the whole world. He drew his breath, frowned, and shouted words. The words screamed their chaos out over the mountaintop and down into the valley: words of forgetfulness, words of deceit. With effort written in the lines of his face he gasped out the last syllables. Then he sank back onto the stone steps.

As sense and reason returned to Waqar's mind, she realised that he had fallen. She got up and climbed up to sit beside him. "Are you all right, my... Atok?" she asked.

"I will be all right," he replied. "If my heart calms down I will be all right." He breathed deeply and slow. "It has been a long time since I used words of such power. I thought I had forgotten."

"What do your words do?"

"They are an illusion, one of my own devising," he replied. "They make this place impossible to find by someone who does not belong here."

"Who belongs here?" she asked.

"Your people, Waqar," he said.

"How long will it last?"

"In theory, forever."

"In theory?"

"This Formula of Words says forever. But hiding something as big as a city is hard and permanence makes it harder. With my failing breath, I would doubt it will last for five hundred years."

It seemed that the whole city had turned out to witness their departure. They loaded their horses and made sure everything was secure.

"Is the old man coming?" Barnabas asked.

"He is saying goodbye to everything he has known for a thousand years," Christopher replied. "I think we can give him a bit of time."

"Look," Philip interrupted, "Here he comes."

The old man was led out by Palla. He smiled when he saw the horses. Philip took the bridle of the largest and led it. "Can you ride?" he asked.

"*It has been a long time,*" the old man replied. He looked over the tack, frowning at the bridle and the bit in the horse's mouth, checking the seat of the saddle and tugging at the stirrups. "*Are these strong enough to support the rider's weight?*" he asked.

"They should be," Philip replied.

"*So you can use them as foot-holds to climb up? I am not as nimble as I used to be.*"

"Of course," Philip agreed. "I will hold the horse's head."

"*There is no need.*" The old man put a hand on the horse's neck and whispered in its ear. "*I am sure she will not give me any trouble.*"

Philip knew he could only understand the old man through some strange enchantment, but it seemed as if the horse understood too. The old man put his hands under one knee and lifted his foot into the stirrup. Then he put his hand up on the saddle-bow and, with an audible grunt, he heaved himself up. He didn't take the reins and he seemed in no hurry to hook his feet into the stirrups. Philip tried to help him find the stirrups but the old man spoke again. "*Leave them,*" he said.

"You seemed to be having some trouble–"

"*I don't trust them,*" he replied. "*If I fall my foot could catch and I could be dragged along.*" Well, Philip had seen it happen, but he didn't want to ride with no stirrups. Then he realised: the old man had never ridden with a saddle. "*Can you help my priestess?*"

"What do you want?"

"Help her up. I want her sitting before me. She cannot ride."

Philip helped her up and the old man put his arms around her on the saddle. *"There,"* he whispered, *"Do you feel safe?"*

"I trust you, my Atok," she replied. *"In your arms I am as safe as I can be."*

They had rode along the mountain range, with the valley on their left, filled with fields and the houses of the farmers and their new Spanish overlords. The old man rode very stiffly but fortunately his horse seemed to be utterly calm. As the trail led them down from the peaks they saw and heard the river ahead of them.

As they picked their way down abandoned roads, Barnabas realised they were never going to return to Cuzco. They had cut off that part of the return journey. He allowed his horse to fall back behind the others. They seemed to be deep in discussion and he reached down to find the little knife in his boot. He picked it up and moved it under his jerkin. He put his hand on the smoothness of the hilt and thought of her.

what do you want she asked in Latin.

"Mistress, we are not going to go through Cuzco. We are about to join the trail beside the river."

which way did you all go

"There is a trail through the mountains."

did you find what you were looking for

"Yes, mistress."

who has it

"Some old man."

is he a magus

"He has less magic than I have, mistress."

good There was a pause. *where are you going now*

"Back to the ocean. The road to Ciudad de los Reyes, mistress."

keep moving and i will catch you on the road

All day they rode, single file along the roads, and by the afternoon they could hear Waqar's Great Speaker again - the river they had crossed coming the other way. Now they were riding a narrow trail between cliffs on one side and a drop on the other. The old man had fallen behind, so Gustavo rode back to find him.

He was sitting on his horse, with Waqar in front of him, looking back along the valley. Far behind them on the road a single file of cavalry was riding hard towards them. Philip shaded his eyes and squinted as Gustavo rode back.

Gustavo squinted too, seeing the glint of the Sun on the armour and trying to pick out the colour of the pennants. "They are two forces," he said. "Some are Don Francisco's livery: king's men."

"And the others?"

"They are the soldiers we saw on Nombre de Dios."

"What about the rider that leads them?"

"The one with the blue cape? I don't recognise him. He is–"

"*It's her,*" the old man said.

"I don't recognise any faces at this distance," Gustavo said.

"*It's her,*" the old man repeated.

Then Gustavo and Philip saw their leader urging them on, brandishing a sword and standing high in the saddle. Sunlight caught the blade and, in a moment of horror, Gustavo recognised that green glint. "Come *ON!*" Gustavo shouted. "We have to cross the bridge!"

Philip rode ahead as Gustavo tried to persuade his horse to turn on the narrow path. They saw as Philip reached the others and John began to lead his horse over the bridge. He put his cloak over the horse's eyes and over they went. Gustavo could see how the bridge sagged as they reached the middle.

As Gustavo reached the bridge Barnabas was just crossing. He dismounted and then waited a moment, trying not to notice how the knots creaked where the rope was tied to the rock. Then he led his horse on to the bridge. He did not want to run but he knew he would not have long. Barnabas was probably frightened, he told himself, but he did seem to be going very slowly.

"Come on!" he heard Christopher shout behind him. "I can see them!"

Gustavo threw his cloak over the horse's eyes and led the horse on to the bridge. He was almost across when he felt the bridge sway as Philip led his horse on. There were two horses on the bridge for a moment but somehow it held. Philip ran across, leading the horse, and Gustavo whispered a prayer for him: if Philip slipped and fell the horse would trample him. Then he looked beyond and saw the riders bearing down on the old man.

Philip hurried by but Gustavo stayed, looking at the old man on the horse, looking back up the path. He seemed to be rooted to the spot, unable to urge his horse on. The rider leading the Spanish stood in the stirrups and raised the long, straight blade that Gustavo remembered from the beach below his grandfather's house. It was her.

Then the old man leaned forward, gathering Waqar with one arm around her, and whispered in the horse's ear. His horse bolted headlong down the trail and straight on to the bridge. Gustavo saw the whites of its eyes and heard the sound of terror it made but it ran straight across the bridge without stopping. He was crouching down to fire his musket at the lead rider when the old man rode past.

"Catch this!" the old man called, and Gustavo looked up.

The old man threw something at him as he passed, and Gustavo dropped the musket to make a good catch. It was a sword, just like the one that the witch was bearing. He expected it to be much heavier than it was. The hilt was gold, with bars enclosing a greenish jewel as big as an egg in a...

"Cut the bridge, you fool!" the old man called back.

Gustavo looked back. The Spaniards had hesitated but their leader was halfway across already, her horse galloping in the sagging middle of the bridge. He saw her helmet was open and he saw her face. He saw the expression change as she realised what he was going to do.

The great blade swept down to cut the rope, and the bridge weaving parted easily before the edge, slicing through in a single sweep. The bridge snaked away, not down, drawing back over the abyss, and Gustavo could see the tension loosed across the span. Eva's horse continued to gallop as the bridge fell away, and for one terrible moment they thought she might carry on. She raised her hand and closed her helm as horse and rider fell and, seconds later, entered the white fury and were instantly lost to sight.

Gustavo gathered up the fallen musket and hastened away from the edge. "Is she dead?" he asked the old man as he climbed up into the saddle.

"She won't be. She will be inconvenienced by the water and she will have lost the horse. But further downstream she will climb out again and make her way back."

"Pity," Gustavo replied, hefting the sword. He was sure it was worth a fortune. The weight of the weapon came from gold wrapped around the hilt, on the end and in a single band below it, and inlaid into the blade along the first third of the length. But the workmanship was like nothing he recognised. The grip was made of metal, not of leather, but the surface was roughened so that it could not possibly slip. A large, slightly greenish gem was on the hilt, clasped in a cage made of six gold bars, and inside it was a dark shadow and a tiny spark of red. The blade was made of green metal, cold as ice, thin as a blade of grass, with a surface so smooth and slippery that it felt soft. But it was not soft: it was hard like diamond and wickedly sharp. Reluctantly Gustavo handed it back to its owner.

"Keep it for now," the old man said. *"When I need it, I will call it to my hand. You are young and strong and it will be better in your hand."* He handed Gustavo a scabbard, rimmed with the same green metal and inlaid with a fortune in gold and jewels.

"Call it to your hand?"

It was as if Gustavo had dropped it. He looked down, at the road and the dirt, but it was not there. He looked up again, at the old man. The old man handed the sword back, carefully, by the hilt.

"How?" asked Gustavo.

"Magic!" the old man replied.

Gustavo put the sword in its scabbard, buckled it on, and attempted to conceal the riches of it beneath his cloak. The old man laughed. Then he leaned over and touched the sword, whispered words, and it was gone.

"Where did it go?" asked Philip.

"I am still wearing it," Gustavo replied. "But we can't see it."

"That is right," the old man agreed. *"I hope you know how to use a sword."*

"I do, sir," Gustavo agreed. "But... not a sword of that design. If you could instruct me then I might be of more use."

"I will see how much I can remember," the old man said.

They were back up in the mountains before they called a halt. Waqar led them into the *tambo* and they made their camp. Gustavo found the old man rubbing down his horse, whispering soothing noises as he did so. The old priestess with him saw Gustavo and turned. The look she gave Gustavo was pure anger. She whispered something to the old man and he turned around.

"What do you want?" he asked.

"This sword, sir," said Gustavo, "Would you show me how to use it?"

"You told me that you know how to use a sword."

"But not of this design."

The old man shrugged. *"I won't teach you with that blade. You will kill yourself. Find two pieces of wood and we will see what you know."*

Gustavo turned and left. "What did he want?" Waqar asked.

"He wants me to teach him sword," the old man replied. "I told him to find wooden sticks."

"He could hurt you."

"I doubt it," the old man smiled.

Gustavo returned with two sticks and passed one to the old man. He held the end of one stick in his fist and raised it to his forehead. *"Come on then,"* he said. *"Show me what you know."*

Gustavo looked at the old man. He was letting the wooden stick trail down by his feet, not guarding himself at all. Gustavo lunged. It seemed the old man vanished. The moment Gustavo had tried to fight the Atlantean witch came flooding back. He stumbled on something and, as he fell, he felt the sharp crack of the wood striking his back. He measured his length headlong in the grass. As he rolled over he saw the stick pointed straight at his face. He spread his hands in surrender and the old man stepped back to allow him to rise.

"Can you teach me?" Gustavo asked.

"What do you want to learn?"

"I... I fought her."

"And you lost, of course."

Gustavo looked the old man in the eye. "Could she be killed with this sword of yours?"

"Of course she could. We are not invulnerable."

"Then teach me to defeat her."

The old man let the tip of his stick swing down to the ground, then leaned his weight on it. *"How long do you have?"*

"I don't know. How long before she climbs out of the river and comes to get us?"

"I don't know. It depends how far ahead of her we get. If she picks up our trail, no more than ten days." The old man sat down. *"I trained alongside her for seven hundred years. Our teacher was the first and greatest swordsman. He was one of a few that had a talent. Their talent is gone out of the world now,* Gustavo. *They are all long dead."*

"Then why did you give me the sword?"

"Because I am not strong enough to fight."

"Then what can I do? Do I have any hope at all?"

"You might be able to surprise her. You are stronger than her and you might be angrier. Give her a moment to collect her thoughts, to say Words of Power, and she will kill you. But take her by surprise and attack with everything you have and you might get lucky." The old man sat down. *"Or, more likely, you will end up dead."*

"Then teach me that."

"Very well. I will do my best."

* * *

After Gustavo had left them and gone to sleep, the old man who was now calling himself Atok sat and watched the stars. The landscape was still brightened by the sharp point of light in Cassiopeia. Waqar sat beside him.

"What are you thinking, my Atok?" she whispered.

"I was just looking at the star," he whispered back. "It has been a long time since I saw one of those."

"I saw you had put it in the heavens for me."

"It wasn't me, Waqar. It is coincidence."

"But I left the temple and walked to—"

"Waqar, it is a star that has flared up. Sometimes they do, like a log splitting in the fire. The insides of stars are so much hotter than the outsides, the brightness of it illuminates the whole... well, it can be seen from a long way away. The light from the star takes many years to get to us. I don't know how far away that is, but most likely this star flared up before I put the first Inka on the throne."

"So what does it mean? Is it to signal the end of our people?"

"It doesn't mean anything, Waqar."

Waqar was silent a while, and he watched her as she stared at the star. Then she turned to him and he saw the starlight glitter off tears of anger in her eyes. "They are destroying everything," she hissed. "The Spanish have killed the last Inka and they make a mockery of his rule – of your laws, my lord – in their lust after gold. And, my lord... I know you are an old man and you won't restore civilisation, but... you let him destroy the bridge."

"It was necessary."

"Men risked their lives to make that bridge, my lord. The penalty for damaging one of the bridges is death."

"Then it is me who deserves to die. I gave the order."

"How could you?"

"It was necessary, Waqar."

"How can it be necessary?"

"Do you know what it is that I carry?"

"I have no idea," she snapped. "I don't understand anything about you."

He smiled back. "You think I am a god, but I am not. I'm just an old man who has learned a few tricks, a few words of a language with which the structure of the universe may be commanded. I was taught by an academy where the guiding principle was ambition. We were all learning power but we did not learn to share power well. Much of our own efforts were diverted into struggling among ourselves, trying to gain power."

"But you brought us civilisation."

"I tried. But... you might be too young to remember... the only reason why the Spanish were able to conquer your people was because the two brothers were fighting to see who would be Inka. That struggle was the opportunity the Spanish needed. They only needed to play one side against the other and then, when the kingdom was all but destroyed by civil war, they took over."

"I know our princes fought. But you are a god. Surely your people would have been wiser than that?"

"We were not, I'm afraid. Where are we now? I hide in mountains and she dares not move openly either. Once we ruled the whole of humanity."

"So you were betrayed by others?"

"I was the betrayer, Waqar. I was the one that destroyed our civilisation. I have seen what happens to ordinary people when a civilisation collapses."

"There must have been some reason, my lord."

"Beyond my anger? I don't think so. When I was a boy and I first came to the City of the Immortals, before I had been there ten years I had killed the... well, our own king's right-hand man. I am the wild dog that bites civilisation, Waqar."

"You said. But why is it necessary to bite us?"

"Because of what I carry. Some kinds of power cannot be shared. The thing I carry is a prison for a spirit that controls the way possibilities become reality. By commanding it I can make anything true. I can change the smallest thing or I can change the greatest thing. The spirit trapped in this thing is as powerful as you imagine me to be."

"Then why not use it to fix things?"

"Because everything is entangled with everything else. Whenever one thing becomes real every other thing in the universe feels it. All the great spirits that run the Universe – and any peasant hedge magician – can tell whenever it is used. The great spirits that run the Universe hate us for imprisoning one of their greatest. And, if I used this thing, every one of them and every magician in the Universe would know it was here on Earth. They would come looking for it."

"But with your power surely you could keep us safe?"

"I could make every magician in the Universe disappear, but many of them are defending us from those great spirits and their armies of monsters."

"Couldn't you defeat the great spirits with your power?"

"They are the foundations on which the Universe is built. If I destroy them I destroy everything."

"Then what can you do? You can't destroy them and you can't fight them?"

"I hoped I could find a way to make peace with the great spirits. But I have not thought of a way in seven thousand years. I have been hiding. This world is a place where the powers of magic are very limited, so that any mages or wild armies would be fighting at a great disadvantage. I have limited things still further in the last few days, so that even spirits will not obey any mortal. They will only obey my own Order."

"But the woman leading the Spanish is one of your Order. She is our enemy."

"Compared to what is out there, she is our friend. What is out there is monsters that hate humanity, hate every one of us, from the highest ranked of our Order to the newborn baby. If they got here they would destroy every one of us, obliterate every shred of human existence from this world. I am dying. I don't want to put this in her hand because I don't trust her. She is insane and her rule would be capricious and cruel. But the powers of the deep Forest would kill all of humanity. And, when I am dead, I will not be able to make any choice. She may be the only one who can save humanity from a Universe that hates us."

"Then what will become of us when you die?"

"I am sorry, Waqar. I don't know. All I can suggest is learning to forgive our enemies. When the monsters attack, we will find that the people we called enemies are the people fighting alongside us. To carry on fighting amongst ourselves when faced with a greater threat would be a fatal mistake."

"Like the empire when the Spanish came?"

"Like that, but with the Spanish as a cannibal horde of monstrous creatures who just want to feast on human flesh."

"Then you are saying I should forgive Gustavo?"

"You should, Waqar. And I hope you can learn to forgive me, too."

Philip wanted to ride hard. The horses were in good condition after a month on the road and, between the mountains and the sea, he felt they were very exposed. Gustavo and John would have encouraged him and even Barnabas, after so much riding, would have been happy. But Christopher would not hear of it.

"The old man cannot manage a faster pace," he said.

"But he can," replied Philip. "Perhaps he is unwell, but see the way the horse responds to him? He is a better horseman than any I have known."

"If he falls and breaks his leg he will not survive," replied Christopher, suddenly flinching as he remembered what he was saying and who he was saying it to. "Then we will be left to face her alone."

"If they catch us out on these plains, then what use do you think he will be?" John asked. "If he is not fit to run what use will he be to fight?"

"Perhaps he will remember some magic," Gustavo suggested.

"He cannot remember any magic," said Barnabas. "Even I have more knowledge than he does. Perhaps he was once the most powerful in the world, but you can see he has forgotten everything."

Waqar leaned a little and turned her head. Her nostrils caught the scent of her husband. *"What are they saying, my Atok?"* she asked.

"I don't know," he replied, looking at them speaking and trying to get some clues from the way their bodies moved. *"I think that they are grumbling about how travelling with an old man is holding them up. They are afraid of what will happen if she catches us here."*

"Can we trust them?"

"I don't think so. But the one called Christopher *is trying to persuade the others to be patient."*

"I trust the one called Christopher *least of all. A man should act like a man. He is like a woman pretending."*

"I think he is a woman pretending. He has been placed under some sort of enchantment that gives him the shape of a man but he still thinks like a woman. He has good control of his face, he is a good actor, but occasionally it slips. You shouldn't let that take away your trust."

"So you trust him?"

"I trust him least of all, but not because of how he acts. I trust him least because I don't know who gave him the body of a man; and because I don't know who taught him to be such a good actor. I am afraid that any person who could teach these things would have to be one of us."

"Like the woman that leads the Spanish?"

"Like her."

"What will you do if she catches us?"

"I will try and talk with her."

"Will that help?"

"I doubt it. But we were friends once – and there will not be any alternative."

They were riding down the valley when they saw the pyramids again. Waqar turned her cheek back to her husband. *"Do you see?"* she whispered.

"It is the temple," he replied. *"It has suffered since I last came here."* He smiled down at her. *"But so have I."*

They rode down and through the space between the pyramid and the houses. Waqar tutted when she saw how the English had left the litter of their camp scattered around, but she remembered arguing with her new husband about the bridge and she left her disapproval unspoken. The English appeared from their hiding places.

"Master Overy," they called out. "Who is that riding with the priestess?"

"A friend," he replied. "He is coming with us to England. We break camp immediately. How soon before the tide is high?"

After they had got down Waqar wandered away. She thought nobody had followed her as she found her way back to the cell where she had lived most of her life. But, as she sat there remembering, the doorway was shadowed.

"My Atok," she said.

"What is this place?" he asked.

"It is where the old priestess put me when I first came here. I have lived here forty years."

"Saying goodbye?"

"We're never coming back, are we?"

"I don't know," he replied. *"Nobody knows what the future holds."*

"I know," she answered. *"I am going to die in a foreign land. But I would rather be there than here, if it is by your side."*

"Waqar, I cannot promise to out-live you. I am dying faster than you are. I think you will be warmed by my own funeral fire."

"Funeral fire?"

"My people burned their warriors. I know it is not what they do here. But... I find I am sentimental."

"I will do that for you, my Atok," she replied, wondering that her voice was still steady. *"Teach me the funeral liturgy of one of your people and I will do it when the time comes. I have conducted your rituals all my life, my lord."*

As soon as the great ocean lifted their boat off the mud, John gave orders and the men heaved at the oars. They slowly moved out into the sea and the crew spread the sails out to catch the wind. They made a wide circle around Ciudad de los Reyes and then turned north, towards Panama and the narrow stretch of land that separated them from the *Dragonfly.*

The old man was sitting in the aft cabin that they had assigned him, with Waqar by his feet. She was spinning thread and he was staring out at the horizon and the trail of disturbed water left behind by their boat. Suddenly the window banged shut. He shifted his weight but she put down her spinning whorl and placed her hand on his knee.

"*You stay still, my Atok,*" she told him in her own language. "*I will open it.*" She staggered a little as the deck shifted, still not confident walking after only a few days at sea. From above them they could hear John's voice, shouting orders, and hurrying feet as the crew hastened to obey.

She opened the window again and the breeze came in, whirling and blowing things in the cabin and splashing her face with water. She tasted the salt on her lips. "*That won't do, my Atok,*" she said. "*I know you say you want draughts, but this is too much even for you.*"

"*I cannot breathe anymore,*" he told her. "*See if you can open it just a little. Fresh air won't kill us.*"

She was trying to figure out how to prop it open just a crack when the door to the cabin opened. The window surged in her hands and banged shut again.

John, Philip, Christopher and Gustavo stood there. "The wind has changed," John said.

"What does it mean?" asked Gustavo.

The old man slowly stood up. Waqar hastened to lend her arm, knowing that a fall could kill him. She helped him as he made his way to the window and opened it. He looked up at the sky and then turned his head sideways, as if he could hear something carried on the wind.

"Barnabas said it was enchantment," said Christopher.

"*Then* Barnabas *is right,*" agreed the old man. "*This wind is not what the spirits of air would choose to do. They are compelled to blow from the south.*"

"It's her," said Gustavo.

"*It is her,*" agreed the old man. "*At the centre of her weather the wind will be stronger.*"

"Then what are we to do?" asked Gustavo.

"We are only four days from Panama," said John. "Less in this wind. If they have just set out then they are more than a week behind us. We will still get away." He turned and went, leading Philip and Gustavo.

Christopher closed the door behind them and then turned back to face the old man. "*What now, my lord?*" he asked. "*Even if she does not catch us on this ocean she will catch us before we get back home. We have to cross the* Atlantic."

"I don't know," the old man replied. *"I am dying. I think you may have chosen the wrong ally."*

"I know we have not chosen the wrong ally, my lord," Christopher replied. *"If it falls into her hands she will bring about the destruction of the world. She would attempt to restore the Land of Immortals and, in doing so, she would draw the monsters of the Forest to Earth. Nothing would be able to stand in their way. Ye have nothing here, in the Sixteenth Century, that could possibly resist that. Ye have no Adepts and ye have no machines. They will trample humanity underfoot. That hasn't happened for nearly seven thousand years."*

The old man smiled, like someone who has learned a secret. Then he said, *"Last time the City put a stop to it."*

"You remember?" Christoper asked, surprise in his voice.

"It was a couple of centuries before I was born," the old man replied. *"Nobody is alive who remembers it."*

"But the City is gone, my lord. With the Mentor gone, with the Gift gone, the City can never return. This thing cannot be allowed to fall into the hands of humanity's enemies."

He found his way back to the bed and sat down. *"You are right,"* he agreed. *"The City is gone and, without the Mentor, it will never return."* He stopped a moment and looked at Christopher, frowning. *"And you are right, the Gift is gone. They were such beautiful people, all of them, and they are all gone."* He looked back and Christopher tried to keep his own emotions under control. The old man sighed. *"We don't have much time, either. She has mastery over the weather and I haven't, not any more. She will catch us."*

"Then what can we do?"

The old man smiled. *"One of the strange things about our science was how little we knew about the bottom of the ocean. It is huge and murky and black. Something as simple as concealment would hide something down there for ever."*

"Like the way you hid the City of the Ancient Peak?"

"Like that."

"Will you do it when the time comes, my lord?"

The old man looked at Christopher and, again, Christopher felt the old man was sharing a secret. *"I will,"* he said. The old man's smile broadened. *"You know,"* he continued, *"When you talk about the Sixteenth Century, you give away a lot about yourself. I believe I know where you come from."*

"Oh," said Christopher Stoke. Waqar and the old man watched the colour spread over his cheeks.

"Don't worry," said the old man. *"Your secret is safe enough with me. I will be dead soon."*

"I don't think so," Christopher assured.

"You know our language, but I think you don't understand who we are."

"I know that yere immortality comes from the way ye breathe. Nobody is sure how it works, my lord, but I am sure yours will recover."

"Once it is gone it does not come back," the old man said. *"I have heard of it returning once, but the person who guided him back to joy..."* He stopped and breathed, a long, deep breath that was interrupted by slight motions like secret sobs. Then he tried again and the breath flowed more freely. *"She was a living miracle, someone who could heal with her voice and her body. But she is gone and nobody will replace her. Certainly not someone like you. I know that you have been trained in some art of the mind, but you can never be the equal of her. As you said, that kind of talent is lost to the world"*

Christopher looked hurt, but then he laughed. *"I know,"* he agreed. *"I'm not a god of medicine. I'm not even* Catherine Howard. *I'm just some ship's surgeon who knows a few healing tricks."*

John went into his own cabin and sat down. Barnabas followed and Philip came after him. Gustavo squeezed in behind them.

"So where are we going?" asked John.

"Panama, of course," said Philip. "We need to make contact with Captain Ranse and get back onto the *Dragonfly*. We need to get back to England before she catches us."

"What will happen when we get back to Captain Ranse?" asked Gustavo. "We will have the whole Atlantic to cross and we will not be able to out-run her."

"We don't need to out-run her," said Philip. "The *Dragonfly* was made by the Hawkins Brothers. In any wind, we can out-manoeuvre the Spanish."

"Never mind that," said John. "Once we are out of sight of land they will not even be able to find us. The ocean is vast and trackless. If we can get away from the coast we will make it back to England."

"I hope you are right," said Philip.

"I hope you are both right," agreed Gustavo.

They all departed, leaving John alone with his charts. A few minutes later the door opened again. John looked up. Christopher came in and sat beside him.

"What do you want?" demanded John.

"I think it might be wise not to share too much of your plans," replied Christopher. "I think it is possible that we have a spy among us."

"I am not concerned about spies," said John. "How would a spy get a message to our enemies? Swim?"

"I think you should be concerned about witchcraft," answered Christopher. "If there was a spy among us they might not have much magic of their own, but it seems to me that their mistress might be able to provide everything they need."

John put down his quill and looked at Christopher. "You are serious?"

"I am. I think it would be best if you didn't share every detail of our planned voyage. It might be best if you told us that you had a different destination to the one you intended."

"I see," said John. "Well, Doctor Stoke, you continue to surprise me."

After Christopher had left John didn't take up his quill. Instead he frowned as he thought. I wonder, he thought. Do we have a spy? And, if we do, who is it?

Barnabas leaned over the rail and looked at the land on the horizon. "I don't see Panama," he said. "Did we navigate wrong?"

"No, Master Saul," replied John. "We navigated right." He cupped his hand to his mouth. "Now listen," he shouted. "This is the end of the voyage. We will be landing here and making our way on foot as soon as we can find our friends the Cimmarones. Let us hope that Captain Ranse can be found when we get to the other side."

The boat was steered towards a sandy shore with the tide running behind her. When they grounded John ordered an anchor and the sails taken in, but the tide was high. As the crew packed their belongings the hull settled into the sand.

Barnabas hid as best he could and found the dagger that she had given him. "Mistress," he thought in his best Latin. "Mistress, speak to me."

what do you want her words replied.

"John Overy tricked me," he admitted. "We are not going to Panama after all. He has beached the boat somewhere and we are all going on foot."

if you have deceived me barnabas saul then your death will be painful and slow

"It is not me, I promise. He said we were going to sneak through Panama."

i will question you when we meet

"Yes, mistress."

what can you see

"Mountains, forest, sea, sand. Nothing else."

that could be anywhere

"I am sorry mistress."

not as sorry as you will be

Barnabas felt the magic fade and he released the hilt of the dagger and concealed it back in his boot. As he did so he remembered the smell of burning flesh and tried not to tremble too much.

— 12 —

Poseidon's Lands

"A sail!" the lookout called.

James Ranse put down his dividers and got up. He went out of the cabin door and climbed the stairs to the quarterdeck. He extended his spy-glass.

"What do you see?" asked Mark Tanner.

"Spanish sail, lad," replied Ranse. "They are in a hurry, too. Something has them riled up." He put the spyglass back in the bag. "Maybe it is this wind," he mused. "It's not natural, not here, at this time of year."

"Will it blow John Overy and his men back home?"

"If they are still alive," Captain Ranse replied. "They are the only reason we are staying on this coast. The Drake Brothers have stirred up a hornet's nest among the Spanish. After we found that merchantman we have a full hold. We just need to return to England but we can't leave until Spring. If John Overy has not returned by then we will have to leave them for dead."

"I think they will return, Captain," said Mark. "Doctor Stoke promised he would take me back to England."

"Don't hope for too much, boy," replied Ranse. "We will look for them before we return, but that won't be for months." He extended the spyglass again and looked at the Spanish in the distance. "There are many of them working along the coast. I think we will need to find somewhere to hide."

The Cimmarones took a winding path down through the forest. While they had climbed the wind had been behind them, blowing rain, but once they were over the pass the weather cleared, the wind dried, and they could see the sea. They had taken far longer than Philip and Gustavo wanted, even before it had been clear that the old man could not climb the mountains that separated the two oceans. They had cut wood and constructed a litter. Now they carried him, strapped to it, with the priestess walking beside him.

"Will he live?" Philip asked Christopher.

"I don't think so," Christopher replied.

"If he dies we will have to take it," Barnabas said.

"We mustn't let her get it," added Gustavo.

"We have to take it to England," said John. "This is too great a matter for us to deal with ourselves."

"What if he dies?" asked Barnabas. "It might be hidden on him so you cannot find it."

"We will take his body back to England, then," said Philip. He turned to Christopher. "Doctor Stoke, how long will he last?"

"I cannot tell," Christopher replied. "After I examined him yesterday evening, I was surprised when he was still alive this morning. I would think it will be days, no more."

"What will we do if she catches us here?"

"We will die," shrugged Gustavo.

John pulled a face. "Then we will have to make sure we get back on the *Dragonfly* and away to sea before she reaches us. Once we are out of sight of land we will be safe. Nobody can track across the blue ocean."

They laboured down the hill, with the priestess fussing every time the litter bumped or swayed too much. Eventually they carried him into a Cimmarone village by the ocean. They were met by the leader of the village.

"Have you seen the English ships?" asked Gustavo.

"One of them sank along the coast," he replied. "But they have been gone through the winter. There are only Spanish boats."

"We have to find them," said John.

"I will send the message up and down the coast," replied the leader.

The Governor of Panama was sitting in his office trying to work. The south wind battered at his shutters, ruining his concentration. The rattling of the shutters meant he didn't hear the knock at his door.

"There's a sail," the messenger called.

"In this weather?" the governor demanded.

"It's Dona Eva's ship."

The governor sprang up and opened the shutters. The wind blew rain into his face, knocking his hat off. He could see down into the harbour where the boats were pitching and rolling on their cables. Beyond the

South Sea heaved in great waves. He saw a ship straining under full sail as it climbed over the crest of one wave, then disappear from view again. He grabbed his cloak and hurried down to the harbour.

By the time he got to the waterfront the gale had almost blown the ship into the harbour. He saw men clinging to the rigging as they fought to reef the sails. Then he saw a blue-cloaked figure on the quarterdeck gesture at the sky and, with a chill on his spine that was nothing to do with the cold, he saw how the clouds rippled and parted in response to that gesture. A single ray of sunshine broke through, illuminating the harbour with vivid, sharp light. As the wind dropped the men hastened to make the ship secure.

The governor ran down to meet Dona Eva. He was joined by the harbour-master. She did not wait for the crew to arrange a gang-plank but jumped straight over the side, landing on her feet on the dock. As she stood her cloak billowed around her.

"Welcome back–" he began.

"Get me horses!" she screamed. "The English have tricked us! They are crossing the isthmus as we speak. We must find them."

The captain of her guard scrambled down the side of the ship and ran over to stand by her side. "Our Lady," he answered, "The land around here is filled with wild men. We cannot simply search it like we would a country tavern. We will–"

"I don't care!" she screamed. "I am not afraid of savages. We will find the English and I will take this thing from them. Then we will rule the world. Are you all too scared of a bunch of savages to take power when you all see it?"

"Our Lady," the captain replied, "Should we make any preparations in case they make it to the other shore?"

"Of course."

"Then I will send word to Nombre de Dios to prepare the *Santa Ana* for sail."

"Make sure you do, Captain," she warned. "I have tolerated too much failure on this journey and my patience is all but exhausted."

"This damned wind," cursed Ranse. The *Dragonfly* was making way through heavy seas. He raised the spy-glass back to his eye and looked at the coast again. He could see the *Cimmarones*, still there, and this time he saw a large, pale man wearing a hat.

"Is it them?" Mark Tanner asked.

"I think that is John Overy, waving," Ranse replied. He raised his voice. "Bill," he shouted, "Get the sails in and the anchor down. And get the boat launched. We will need to fetch them in the boat."

"That will be hard rowing," said Mark.

"Aye, lad," agreed Ranse, "But with the wind blowing from the North we cannot put in. We need sea room. If we put in we will be trapped on shore."

It was hard rowing and Ranse watched with frustration as the boat pitched through the waves. He felt exposed, knowing that the *Dragonfly* was visible but that they couldn't flee Spanish attack without abandoning the crew of the longboat. It was a risk and Ranse hated risk.

But eventually the boat made it back to the ship. John Overy, Philip and the Spaniard were working hard at the oars with the other men, and Christopher Stoke threw the rope to haul the boat in. The crew came aboard readily enough, but they left two additional passengers with Christopher in the boat. James looked down at the little brown woman and the old man with suspicion.

"Is your passenger going to stay in the boat forever?" he called down to Christopher.

"He is sick, Captain," Christopher called back. "He will need to be helped."

The crew let down a rope with two loops in it and Christopher got the loops around the old man's chest and under his hips. Then they hauled him aboard. Palla fussed but Christopher was able to calm her down.

Ranse shook his head and turned to John. "Where did you find him?"

"In the mountains," replied John. "He has... the thing that Master Horsey sent us to find."

"Really? That is all we came to find?"

"I don't understand it either," John agreed. "But I have seen a lot of strange things I don't understand."

"Like the star?"

"Captain Ranse," Philip interrupted, "We have to get going. She is right behind us."

"She?" asked Ranse.

"Gustavo's enemy."

"Where are we going?" asked Ranse.

"England," replied John.

"In January?" demanded Ranse. "John, you know what the sea is like around England and France in January. One day could be fair weather but next day could bring a storm that would batter us to pieces. It is far too great a risk."

"There is no help for it," said Philip. "We have been running headlong since we left the City of the Ancient Peak and we have very nearly been caught. If she catches us she will torture and kill us all."

"If she catches us then she will change the course of history, Captain Ranse," added Christopher. "The struggle between Protestant and Catholic will become irrelevant. It will be a struggle of her and her magicians against the whole of the wild forest. Ordinary people like you and me will be annihilated."

"We can lose her in the ocean," said John.

"I don't believe it," answered Christopher. "I don't believe we can lose her. We have to make a stand. We don't need to worry about weather because she controls the weather. We just need to out-run her until we get to England. Then, in England, we will make a stand."

"We can only out-run a Spanish ship of that size if we sail across the wind," Ranse said. "If she controls the wind we will never get away from her. On a downwind run the designs of the Hawkins Brothers won't help us. The ship that carries the most sail will run the fastest. Downwind, we cannot out-run a galleon in the *Dragonfly*."

"We must try," said Christopher.

"We will try, Doctor Stoke," agreed Ranse. "But if she truly controls the weather we will not succeed."

Jane Fisher's Diary,
Somewhere in the Atlantic,
8 January 1573 (Julian Calendar).

I remember telling Edward and James that I had never lost a patient and it fills me with shame. Even if I could forget that I lost seventeen of them I know now that I am going to fail. The old man is dying and there is nothing that any of us can do. I have seen the way their immortality fills them with life and vigour. I know that his presence should fill a girl with fear and admiration, but his presence is not there. It is as if he has already gone and, like a decapitated chicken, his body is merely carrying out reflex functions until it finally falls over for the last time.

And he is the only hope we had of protecting ourselves from the dread mistress that is coming. Her ship is driven by winds that we know will never fail. Ranse promised us that the English ships would always out-manoeuvre the Spanish, but when the Spanish control the weather that is no longer true. She will catch us up in only a few hours, she will come aboard with her troops and she will slaughter us. Then she will take it and change the world.

That's it. I'm never going home. Everything I have ever loved is never going to be.

"Sail!" called the lookout.

"What?" yelled John. "We're in the middle of the ocean."

Ranse came up the stairs from the cabins. He got out his spy-glass and scanned the horizon. "She's Spanish," he said. "A three-master."

"Is it the *Santa Ana*?"

"It could be," Ranse replied. He thought a moment. "John, turn us West by North West."

John bellowed orders and the crew scrambled up the rigging to re-set the sails. As they did he turned the wheel and the boat slowly turned to port. A minute later the *Dragonfly* was sailing neatly across the wind.

"We're heading towards them," said Philip.

"We will pass them before they can get to us," replied John. "And when we've passed them they will be downwind of us and can never catch us."

But the Spanish galleon simply turned towards them. They did not bother to re-set the sails. Minutes later the sails on the Dragonfly began to flap. "What is the matter?" asked Philip.

"The wind's changed," grumbled John. "Captain?" he shouted.

But Ranse was already coming back up the stairs. "John, we need to get upwind of that Spaniard. Steer a course South-West."

John turned the wheel and the *Dragonfly* turned, now pointing back in the direction she had come. Ranse stayed on deck as the wind followed them again. They circled right around the Spanish ship, but the wind was always behind the Spaniard and they were gaining.

Philip, Christopher, Gustavo and Barnabas came up on deck. "What is happening, Captain?" Philip asked.

"It's this infernal wind," Ranse cursed. "Whichever way we turn it follows, blowing that Spaniard towards us."

"Can they catch us?" Christopher asked.

"If the wind keeps favouring them, they can," Ranse replied. "We can cross the wind and even beat against it, but they are rigged for downwind. They carry more sail than us. If the wind stays behind them they will catch us. The wind has blown all around the compass to keep them following us."

"Do you see her?" Barnabas asked.

Ranse leaned closer. "In the glass I see a woman with armour and a blue cloak in the wind."

"That's her," Barnabas agreed.

"I will not have that shouted to the crew, Master Saul," Ranse ordered. "We do not need to tell them that a witch controls the wind."

"They will know soon enough," Christopher said.

"They know now," Barnabas said. "You are an educated man, Captain, but common people are not stupid."

Gustavo put his hand on the hilt of the old man's sword. "If we are going to have guests we should prepare them a welcome."

"We will not discuss this on deck," said Ranse. "John, take the wheel. Try and keep circling around them. The rest of you, come to my cabin."

They came into the captain's cabin and they sat down. The boat rolled as John changed direction but, in the small space, any of them could reach out and steady themselves against the walls or the table.

"What do you think we should do next?" asked Ranse. "If they really control the wind, then they will catch us very soon."

"She controls the wind," affirmed Barnabas. "We cannot escape her."

"Will they accept surrender?" asked Ranse. "The men that Drake had to put ashore were ill-used by the Spanish."

"We cannot expect any mercy from her," replied Christopher. "She is insane. But, gentlemen, it is too late to think of our own lives. The only thing that is important is to prevent her from gaining the thing she seeks."

"You despair of our lives very lightly, doctor," said Philip.

"I don't despair of our lives, but I know what it is we were sent to fetch. It cannot fall into her hands." He frowned a moment as he thought of persuasive words. "For her to get hold of it would mean the defeat of every Protestant nation in Christendom."

"It means that much?" asked Philip.

"Do you think she would risk so much to find it if it wasn't important?"

"So putting it out of her reach will hurt her?" Gustavo asked.

"It will frustrate her intensely," replied Christopher.

"Then we should do it," Gustavo answered. "And, if we die afterwards, I am sure God will take care of us."

"It is true," agreed Philip. "We should do what we should and trust God for the rest."

"How do we put it out of her reach?" asked Ranse. "Would it be enough simply to throw it overboard?"

"It should be," answered Christopher. "He has used his words of... his magic spells to prevent it from being discovered. All we need is to throw it overboard and it will sink to the bottom of the sea."

"But if she is such a powerful witch, won't she be able to fetch it?" Barnabas asked.

"Not according to him. We talked about it. Although she might be able to walk on the bottom of the sea she cannot find it. The bottom of the sea is dark and the ocean is murky. The sea-bed lies more than a league beneath us. Even if she could walk on the bottom, she would have to search for it on her hands and knees, in the dark, by fingertip. And the thing she would be groping for in the dark is concealed by magic. She would never find it."

"When did you become an expert in magic, doctor?" asked Ranse.

"I am no expert in magic," replied Christopher. "But I speak the old Atlantean and I understand what he says."

"How did you learn that?" asked Barnabas.

"You would be amazed at the things I learned in University," Christopher smiled. "But we should get started. We haven't much time."

The two ships drew closer and closer. The Spanish soldiers could be seen on the decks and Ranse ordered chain shot. The decks of the Spanish ship were far above the guns of the little English boat. The seas were pitching both ships about and one of the risks was that the waves would smash the two ships together. As the ships pitched, Ranse suddenly called "Fire!"

The guns roared, the ship jumped, and powder-smoke billowed over the decks. As the wind whipped the smoke away, they saw his plan. The decks of the Spanish ship, with the men waiting to board, were smashed to chaos. Firing at the top of the ship's roll, their shot had gone high into the upper decks of the other.

But from the quarterdeck of the *Santa Ana* the witch ran forward, her sword raised above her head, and called to her men. The waves lifted the Spanish ship and then the other, and then as they both descended they were tipped together. For a moment, the Spanish ship could be seen under the English sails, wood moving behind wood, and then the two ships came together with a sound of tearing timbers. Grapples flew and then the Spanish soldiers were among the English. Muskets and pistols fired, from both sides, and then it was swords and knives. Over the sounds of the ships and the sea, the ring of metal on metal could be heard, and the screams of men killing and dying.

Waqar heard the screams and the roar of the guns. She sat on the edge of her king's bunk and she found her stone knife as the door opened.

"*Be calm, mistress,*" Christopher told her in Quechua.

"*What is happening?*" she screamed.

"*We need to relieve him of his burden, Mother.*"

Waqar brandished the knife. "*Stay away from him,*" she warned. "*I won't let you steal anything.*"

"*Mother, listen to me. The thing he carries will kill him, even if she doesn't take it from him first. The god he used to be when he was young, she is that and more. He cannot resist her and nobody and nothing else on this boat can help. He will die if he does not let it go. I am not trying to steal from him. I am trying to save his life. You have to believe me, Mother...*"

"*No,*" Waqar replied, pointing the knife. "*We have been tricked and cajoled by you foreigners for too long.*"

"*Look at him, Mother. Look at his blue eyes and his white hair. He is a foreigner too.*"

"*He is my husband and I will protect him with my heart's blood.*"

Philip came through the door. His rapier was in his hand and the blade was smeared with red. "She isn't convinced, is she?" he asked.

"Try to be understanding–" Christopher began.

"She is in the foc'sle, Doctor. We don't have time for understanding, do we?"

On the decks, desperation ruled. The Spanish soldiers were trained professionals but unused to fighting on the pitching decks, while the English were untrained pirates fighting for their lives. Then, through the din, her high clear voice rang out. "To me, my knights!" And there she was in the forecastle of our boat, a tall female figure in her shining green armour. A sword was in her hand, not the rapier of the modern gentleman but a great green glaive, a weapon that Gustavo knew would cut through steel or wood, through flesh or bone without mercy. The crew knew the dread of that sword, but Gustavo knew it better, for he had its brother in his hand.

With one hand on the rail of the quarterdeck, blocking the way to the cabins, and the other hand raising that blade high, Gustavo called out his defiance. "To me, Englishmen. Do not be so afraid of a woman." Then, in Spanish, "*Come on, witch! See, my sword is the equal of yours and my desire for vengeance will never be defeated! Perhaps you would like to practice sword now!*" It was utter bravado, his inflamed blood giving voice. The crew came to him, gathered around with their courage returning.

But she came on. A wedge of her caballeros followed her, down from the forecastle and across the main decks. An unfortunate crewman, Mark the Tanner's Son, got in her way and tried to threaten her with a knife. She slashed across, cutting him through the elbow, through his body and out through his other upper arm. The arms fell away, and for a moment his face registered the purest terror, before his body fell apart onto the wet decks. She did not break her stride. The other crewmen cowered as they saw his death and Gustavo knew that their nerve would not last long.

Philip came out of the cabin and called, calmly but urgently: "I cannot find it, Gustavo. Palla is ready to kill us all, the old man won't awake and I cannot find it."

"You must keep looking", Gustavo told him. Then he remembered how the old man had hidden the sword with a touch. "He's wearing it, but you can't see it. Use your touch." Gustavo could see that Philip had no idea what he was talking about. "Look, just throw him over. If he wakes, fine – if not, he'll weight it into the deeps. We don't have time!"

"She's coming up the stairs," yelled Ranse, on the deck above.

"Do it!" Gustavo commanded Philip. He turned to the approaching figure and shouted in Spanish. "*Hey! Witch! Are you still trying to persuade me to marry you?*"

"*You young fool!*" she shouted back as she climbed the steps, "*I am coming to kill you!*"

Then, before he had time to think how stupid he was being, he ran at the witch woman, sword first.

As she came up over the ladder leading down to the main deck, Gustavo's borrowed sword struck her helmet over the ear. The point skidded off the metal, like ice or glass, but her head was knocked sideways. An instant later he slammed into her, body to body, and carried her over the rail and over the side of the boat. He held on to her as he looked down at the ocean. For an instant his mind thought of the abyss that Barnabas had assured them was below the surface, a league or more down into the darkness. With a sharp tug, she got one arm free, and as she reached out her fingers, her sword appeared from nowhere. Then they hit the water.

Gustavo had never been a strong swimmer. His mother and his nurse both believed that entering the water was a challenge to the spirits of river and ocean. He was told as a child that these spirits would suck out his eyes and feast on his entrails if he ever entered the ocean.

The water was clear and his eyes were open. From below the surface he saw the hull of the boat, still sailing past, and the surface like a glittering silver mirror all shivered to pieces. Below them was the deep blue that covered the abyss, three thousand fathoms and more of black water. His ears were full, making sounds distant as if heard along a long tunnel, and she was holding him down. Gustavo swung the sword, but the blade was turned sideways by the water, making the blow ineffective. She swung back at him, with the same result. Then she dropped her sword and it reappeared in her hand facing the other way, ready to stab.

Looking up at her preparing to kill him he remembered his own Eva, in Heaven, waiting. It felt like coming home.

"They're in the water," John shouted at the cabin door.

"Well, that buys us some time," Philip said. "Gustavo said that I should–"

"It won't buy us any time at all," Christopher argued. "She will kill him and then she will climb back on board." He got one hand free of Waqar's struggling form and grasped her throat. *"I'm sorry, mother,"* he whispered, and his fingertips found the places on her neck. He lowered her to the ground quickly but gently then stepped over her. "Get the window open," he ordered Philip. "Then come and help me."

Below the water, with his lungs ready to burst, Gustavo felt rather than heard an impact. He saw the silver of the surface explode into foam, with a sound like a million tiny bells. Below the foam, the old man was sinking. Philip had thrown him out of the cabin window.

One hand of hers still held him down, the other ready to stab him through with her terrible sword, but she'd forgotten Gustavo already. Her helm was turned to look at the old man in the sea. He had the jewel in his hand and, as they watched, he dropped it. It fell through the water for maybe a second or two, the chain swirling above it as it sank, before it vanished from sight into the dark.

She released Gustavo and she kicked off, descending through the water. The old man looked down, apparently unconcerned, then began to swim towards Gustavo, just as he managed with an effort to get his face into the cool air. Gustavo gasped and gasped, filling his aching lungs. As he inhaled, a wave rode over his head, filling his throat and nose. He went down again.

An arm brought him back to the surface. The old man was lifting Gustavo's head on his chest. He turned and began to swim on his back, slowly but steadily, towards the boat.

All eyes watched the water. At the bows of the *Dragonfly* the invaders crammed the rail and at the stern the defenders also watched. They saw Gustavo drowning and the old man rescuing him. They also saw her armoured form clambering up the side of the Spanish galleon, her feet and hands apparently sticking to the wood as if she was an insect. As they saw her climb over the side she raised her visor and shouted down at them.

"You are fools, all of you!" she screamed in Spanish. *"We will meet again and I will teach you all the price of your folly."*

Then she stepped back from the rail and they could no longer see her. The Spanish hurried back to their ship.

Barnabas saw that all eyes were on her. He reached into his boot-top and pulled out a dagger. He reached out and dropped it over the side of the boat.

The old man dragged Gustavo to the *Dragonfly* and strong hands reached down to pull them to safety. They hauled Gustavo and the old man out from the ocean and carried them onto the deck. The old man was huddled and shivering.

"Bring him into the cabin," commanded Christopher. He was still weak and cold. Christopher gave him brandy while the priestess helped him to get dry.

"It is gone," said the old man, reaching for his neck. *"So far below the water, lost with Words of Misdirection, it will be out of her reach."*

Christopher swallowed and paused a moment. *"Good,"* he replied, with relief. Then he said, *"Let me offer you something to replace it."*

The old man's look to Christopher was dismissive but he said nothing. Christopher reached around his own neck and found a chain there. He drew out a small gold object and opened it. It was a locket shaped like a heart. *"I brought this for you,"* Christopher said, opening it and offering it to the old man.

The old man took it, disinterestedly. He looked down. Opened, the locket showed two tiny portraits. The faces of two young women looked out, their heads slightly turned towards each other. The one on the left had pale blonde hair and a strong nose that told of nobility rather than of prettiness. The other was the opposite, with a nose that turned up like a little girl's, peppered with freckles and framed by hair of red gold.

He looked up, with a face that was eager and perhaps accusing. *"Where did you come by this?"* he demanded.

"I cannot tell you that," Christopher replied. *"But it is a much lighter burden. It is harmless, no more than it seems: a little box on a chain containing two portraits of pretty women. I thought you would like it."*

He looked down at the portrait on the right and then up at the ship's physician. *"Harmless,"* he laughed. *"If only you knew."* He put the chain around his neck, then stared at the two pictures for a long time, breathing deep, relaxed breaths. *"I like it,"* he answered at last. *"Now leave me."*

Christopher went out to see who needed his healing. The old man snapped the locket shut and hid it, before Waqar could see what was inside it.

Above decks the men struggled to separate the two ships. The Spanish helped them with shoves from their own boat. The Spanish ship turned East and the men shook out ragged sails. The galleon pulled away from the English barque and began the long trek to the horizon.

With Ranse guiding and John shouting at them, the crew of the *Dragonfly* lifted a yard as the new mast and rigged what sails they could. The cold winter winds of the Ocean of Atlantis filled the sail and the hull began to make way through the water.

Ranse turned the wheel, looking at the compass and then up to the sky. But many of the men could also look at the sky and see what heading they were steering. The *Dragonfly* was going home.

At the Sign of the Seven Stars

Crossing the Atlantic was easy as the wind blew steadily from the West. They had sailed for four weeks when they first saw land. The cry from the rigging brought them all up on deck. Ranse took out his spy-glass and looked along the coastline.

"I don't recognise it," he said. "I don't think it is Ireland."

John stood by his elbow. "It is too green for Spain," John said.

Philip and Gustavo joined them. "This could be where you get off," said Ranse.

"If this is France, that is," Philip replied. "I need to join Francis Walsingham in Paris."

Barnabas looked around cautiously as the old man shuffled across the deck, supported by Waqar on one side and Christopher on the other. *"Land,"* he said to Captain Ranse. *"It has changed since I last saw it."*

"You know where that is?" Ranse asked.

"I do, but I don't know what you people call it. If you have a map I can point to where we are. Or..." his face creased in a frown. He breathed in, deeply, then said strange, twisted words. Before them the shapes of a coastline appeared, floating on the air between them.

Ranse jumped back. "Witchcraft!" he exclaimed.

"It is a simple illusion," the old man smiled. *"The mainland south of the Archipelago turns around a headland."* He indicated what was obviously the west coast of France. *"This island here used to be joined by a beach to the mainland. In the shelter of the island there was a settlement. It was the local community centre for this coastline. My people lived here: the Sea People."*

"They still do," said Ranse. "Behind the island there is a port called Trinity." He turned to John and pointed. "Can you get the lads ready, John? We will steer south of that island there and then into the port."

"Aye," replied John. He hastened off to rouse the crew.

Ranse turned to Philip. "You need to get ready," he said. "We will get fresh water here and the crew can spend a night ashore. But, after this, our next port will be London."

The old man found a spot on the quarterdeck to sit and Waqar and Christopher helped him.

"*When you get to London you will need English names,*" said Christopher in the Quechua language.

"*The only name I want a foreigner to call me is mistress,*" said Waqar.

"*Well, mistress sounds almost like an* English *name. You will be all right.*"

"*She has named me, too,*" agreed the old man. "*She calls me her little fox.*"

"*Little?*" laughed Christopher.

They both laughed back. "*So what is a fox in your language?*" Christopher asked.

"*Atok.*"

"*That is not your native language, á Uasal.*"

"*Oh.* Sionnach, *then. But I told her 'fox' because she doesn't know what a wolf is. A wolf cub would be* coileán."

"Colin *is an* English *name.* Colin *and* Paula Wisdom. *You will be all right.*"

"Colin Wisdom," the old man repeated, trying to get the vowels right.

"Paula," Waqar said.

"*You both should practice your English more,*" added Christopher. "*I know your enchantment works,* Master Colin, *but intelligent people will spot it. You saw* Captain Ranse *respond to your illusion. Magic is illegal in England.*"

The *Dragonfly* rounded the island and into the port of Trinité sur Mer. They docked and the harbour-master came aboard. He came on to the quarterdeck, looking surly, and addressed them in French.

"We are English," Captain Ranse said, slowly. "This boat, the *Dragonfly*, belongs to Edward Horsey, Governor of the Isle of Wight."

"*Some of them are* English," the old man added.

The harbour-master smiled at last. He addressed the old man in another language, one that none of the rest of them recognised. "*Where are you from, then?*" he asked.

"*From the Land of Immortals,*" the old man replied. "*Once this coast, from the Inland Sea to the Archipelago, belonged to my people.*"

"*Before the Romans came?*" asked the harbour-master.

"*Six thousand years ago,*" the old man said. "*I don't know anything about* Romans."

"Well," the harbour-master answered. *"Welcome home, my lord."*
"We would wish that our visit be kept secret," said the old man.
"Don't worry, my lord, it will be."

They were drinking in a waterside bar in the port, enjoying the way the floor beneath them did not move. The English crew had found drink and local girls and were singing their relief at a successful voyage. Ranse had found a table separate from the crew, and was drinking with John, Christopher and Philip. They had even made Barnabas welcome. But Christopher watched another table, where the old man he had named Colin was drinking with the old woman he had named Paula.

He saw Gustavo come in, followed by a local girl. He could see that Gustavo was rejecting the girl's advances. He picked up his mug and stood. "Excuse me, gentlemen," he said. He threaded his way through the dancing crowd towards Gustavo. The local woman was speaking angrily.

"Excuse me," Christopher said to her in French. *"My friend has recently been widowed. He is not ready for love yet."*

She glowered but she stopped arguing. Then, as she looked into Christopher's face, her anger receded. *"Pardon me,"* she said. She looked at Gustavo. *"I hope your heart heals soon."* She turned away and entered the crowd of dancers.

"Thank you," said Gustavo in Spanish. "That was hard. She is pretty enough, but–"

"But she is not your love."

"Well, she isn't."

They went over to the tap-man and Christopher found a drink for Gustavo. They leaned on the wall and looked at the crowd. "You will get well," Christopher promised. "You will never forget her, but grief passes."

"Did I avenge her? I am not sure."

"You did, Gustavo. She has planned to get that thing for thousands of years and you took it away from her."

"It feels like nothing," Gustavo whispered. "I feel like nothing."

"That is grief, Gustavo. It will pass."

"I don't think I can ever love again."

Christopher nodded in the direction of the old man called Colin drinking with his wife called Paula. "You think you cannot learn to love again? Look at him. He thinks that everyone he has ever loved is dead. That is a lot of people, Gustavo: he is nearly seven thousand years old. You see the way he has his arm around her? He looks after people and for that they love him."

"It is easy for him. She thinks he is a god."

"He and his like are close enough to gods that it hardly matters. And yet he was dying, Gustavo. People will always find reasons to love. She has lived with solitude for decades and yet she gives her heart. And he has lived with solitude for centuries."

"Why hold hands when the hand in yours will only be torn away?"

"How many hands have been taken from his? We give and receive love because it is love that gives life meaning. A held hand in the darkness is all there is, Gustavo. Do not scorn it because you know it will not last forever."

"She was stolen from me."

"Our lovers are always stolen from us. I know she was taken too soon, but remember the wedding vows: *'til death us do part.* Even if we live out our natural spans, we are still separated by death. Nothing is forever."

"She promised me forever, Christopher."

"I know she did. She believed it, I am sure. But the thing she was promising you is something that she had not the power to grant. Nobody has the power to grant that."

"So you are saying that love is fragile?"

"Love is as frail as the human condition, Gustavo. If you love you will lose love. But if you don't love you will not save your heart, because the passage of time will take everything away from you anyway. Life is like a stream. You can never step into the same stream twice, for the water you remember has flowed away, but you can drink as deep as you wish." Christopher turned to Gustavo, and raised his mug. "So drink deep, Gustavo, while you still have the chance."

It was close to midnight and the summer stars looked down on the plain. It was the Eve of St. John and no right-thinking person would dare to approach the Giant's Dance on such a night. The stones stood or lay on a slight rise that gave them vantage across the whole valley: a reminder that behind and beneath the bright new ideas of modern thought older, darker truths remained.

A single figure walked in the darkness, a few possessions on his back. His clothes were that of a man of quality, but they were stained by salt water and faded by the tropical Sun. His walk was weary but eager, like the walk of a pilgrim. Eventually he reached the top of the incline and entered the ring of stones. He swung the pack off his back and sat on one of the stones that had fallen. He looked up at the Moon, and then over to the new star, faded now but still visible among Cassiopeia's W-shape of stars. He tried to judge the hours by looking at the Pole Star. The Little Dipper could be used as a clock, but only as an hour-hand that moved at half speed. It must be nearly midnight, he thought. He knew how to sit alert and empty his mind of distractions.

Another light in the sky caught his attention and, as he got to his feet, his heart raced. This star was descending, falling silently out of the sky towards him. He picked up his pack. A brilliant beam of light appeared suddenly, illuminating the stones of the Giant's Dance. The man who had been calling himself Christopher Stoke raised his hand to shade his eyes. The craft that descended towards him was shaped like a corpulent disc, with a bubble on the top and fins at the back. It landed in front of him and the rear opened, part going up and part going down to form steps.

"God's wounds,'tis good to see thee!" the traveller exclaimed.

The pilot remained at the controls but her companion stood on the steps and reached out a hand to welcome the traveller in. The companion was a tall woman with tightly-curled dark blonde hair and blue-green eyes. "How was it, Jane?"

"I am *not* doing that again," Jane Fisher replied. "And the sooner you can get me out of this ridiculous body the better I will like it."

The pilot turned back to the controls and the craft closed again. Then with a simple movement she guided them out into the sky, back among the stars. "We are clear of Earth," the pilot said. "We'll get you back to the future soon, Doctor Fisher."

"We will be home soon," her companion agreed. "But, if you are really that impatient..." She touched Christopher Stoke and whispered Words of Power. The shape of Christopher's body flowed and melted, softened and curved, returning to her true form.

"Home is where I will stay," Jane said, wriggling where her clothes were too tight or not supportive enough. "I don't care what incentives you offer, *Uasal Eibheara*, or what threats you make. I am not coming back. I quit. If I have learned one thing, it is this: history belongs in books."

The pilot moved the controls and the stars blurred and vanished.

"Hey, Anne," he roared, "Don't leave a gentleman waiting in the commons! Bring him through!" The girl flinched at the loud, slightly foreign voice.

Gustavo did not recognise her. He smiled at her. "Don't worry, he's not as frightening as all that." She made no reply, now overcome with shyness, but led them through in silence to where the caller waited. He was a big, tall man, his face lined and framed with close-cropped white hair, but he was hale and strong, with both power and mischief in his blue eyes. His wife looked through from the bar, a tiny woman with iron-grey hair and dark eyes.

"Sort this new girl out, eh?" he called to her, then added in Quechua, *"but be kind, my little white egret."* She smiled back and disappeared back into the commons. The big man cleared maps from the table, pulled up a chair, and sat down with Queen Elizabeth's Astrologer. "So, Doctor Dee, what brings you to this part of London?"

"Apart from your fine ales?" Dee didn't know how to talk to this man. He looked around, as if he might be overheard. "I have not been told the whole story of what happened on Gustavo's visit to the New World, but some of the things I have heard, particularly from Barnabas, are more than a little intriguing. I have tried not to meddle too much in your affairs, but I can see that some of the stories I have heard have a foundation in truth."

Gustavo could see Colin adopting his guarded face, the one he used when Walsingham or Burghley came to visit. "Tell me these... stories."

"Barnabas told me that when he was captured in Nombre de Dios, he spoke to a Spanish lady who claimed to be an ancient sorceress. She offered to teach him the secret of eternal life. She offered him the Philosopher's Stone, if he would only lead her to a certain person or secure for her a certain treasure."

"Go on." Colin was all ears, and the way he sat suggested a certain alertness that Gustavo had learned to fear. In a heartbeat, that terrible sword Gustavo had wielded that cold day on the Atlantic could be in his hand and, before the heart had a chance to beat again, Dee would be dead. The man who called himself Colin was now Gustavo's teacher and he had learned to fear him.

"I have noticed, Magus, that your health has improved considerably after your return to London. When you arrived, you were an old man, confined to a sickbed that seemed likely to become a deathbed, attended by a woman who was your nurse but the right age to be your daughter." He stopped, looking for some kind of recognition or acknowledgement, but none came. He plunged on. "Now, five years later, the change is remarkable. Your nurse is now a wife who is perhaps a little older than you. You appear like a man of perhaps fifty years. Your strength and vitality is talked of by the people who have seen it and there are rumours that you can throw out any drunken braggart who offends you, be he alone or even in gangs.

Your house is frequented by the sailors who go on account and they are not gentle folk." He had another sip of his ale, perhaps to wet his drying and tightening throat. "They also rumour that angels inhabit this house."

"And, Doctor, why are you interested in these rumours and speculations?"

"Because if these are true, and I believe them to be true, then you are the greatest magician in Britain since Merlinus graced Arthur's Court."

"And if I were the Merlin to Elizabeth's Arthur, what then? Where is Morgana?"

"I suspect Morgana is in Spain."

"And would we want her to know I was here?"

"No, you wouldn't, and the best Queen's Magician would be an old fool who fancies he speaks with angels and knows a little of mathematica and the science of the mariner. Someone to distract the eye, like a stage trick that the audience stares at while the real machinery that makes them gasp works unseen. And the only people at the Court who would know the difference would be gentlemen like Walsingham or Lord Burghley."

"And what would be the likely outcome if the old fool figured it out? A visit to Tyburn, perhaps?"

Gustavo could see fear in the doctor's eyes, but also he could see something else, something stronger. It was the hunger for knowledge. "The old fool might visit the Magus and ask him to teach. Perhaps I have some small ability and with tuition might better learn to serve my Queen and country."

"Didn't you teach Barnabas Saul?"

"I did," Dee replied. "But the language of magic does not work anymore. By the time he returned we could no longer work it."

"That is for your own good: your own good and that of everyone in the world. I can't teach you what you cannot learn. Until we can end our power struggle and I can... repair another injustice, it is for the best."

"Magic isn't the only thing you know, Magus."

"You want to live forever?"

"Many people want to live forever, Colin Wisdom."

"Of course. But I believe you are too late. My tuition started when I was a boy. I took forty-seven years to begin to master it, and I was considered to be an exceptional student. Only one student had learned it before me and he didn't see his third century. I don't think you have forty years to learn to live forever." He looked old for a moment then talked much more quietly. "I have been teaching Paula and I have been teaching Gustavo. I think Gustavo might have time to learn, but it is too soon to tell. I never tried to teach it before and our teacher did not share all his secrets. Gustavo bears his own portion of anger and grief. I have seen anger and grief slow down a student's ability to learn immortality. Paula will not learn in time – perhaps the discipline will give her another ten years, but perhaps it won't. She is going to die." He looked more lonely than ever. "I have not had a companion for many generations."

He thought of it, then laughed, spoke quietly, perhaps hoping Gustavo wouldn't hear what he already knew. "My last companion now calls herself 'Eva de Castilla'," he confided, "And last time we met she tried to kill me. Our Order, the Sea People, did not marry. From my earliest days in what you call Atlantis I was taught that Atlanteans do not live forever. Even my childhood friend ran away into a world of rousing music and impossible dreams before I got the chance to tell her what I felt. Or even recognise it myself. Now, I think I will lose Paula after only a few short years." He breathed in, and breathed out again, a long sigh that seemed to let out a great sadness. Then he smiled, adjusted the mask on his expressions. "I don't want to live forever. I have lived far too long but I don't age because I have too much work to do. And I doubt you can learn in time. If you really want to try, you can. But there is a price, a price you will owe to me, as well as the weariness and sorrow that immortality will inevitably bring you." He watched Dee, to be sure that he wanted to pay the price. It seemed that he wanted to pay any price. "I will try and teach you: I will not promise that you will learn. In exchange, you will swear your life in fealty to me: and I will enforce that oath with forbidden magic."

Dee nodded assent. "What do you want from me?" he asked.

"Service, of course. But the first thing is that I would like to use your library."

"What are you looking for?"

"I am looking for others of my kind. When your servant found me in the Western Land I thought – I hoped – I was the last one left. But I was mistaken. You mentioned Merlin and, I believe, with his associations with Avalon, he was one of us. Not one of the Chosen but one of our number nevertheless. Morgana is definitely our Eva of Castile. I would like to identify where the rest of our Chosen Circle went but, much more importantly, I need to find the king, our Teacher. When I have become strong again I can face Eva, but I may never be strong enough to face our Teacher. He taught us and even three of us may not have defeated him. It may be that the Chosen Circle cannot defeat him because there are not enough of us left. What I am trying to do is find him, by looking for legends about old kings, gods, or magicians. She is doing the same thing, through the Inquisition, but her Inquisition drives the Midsummer People away. They are my children and they are my main source of information.

But I need your library."

Dee looked puzzled. "Who are Midsummer People?"

Colin Wisdom called out in a strange tongue. Then he added, "Madimi, show yourself to them. They are safe people."

From a corner of the room, near the door, a child's voice spoke, in accented English. "Hello, doctor," she said. He looked around. A child of perhaps seven years was there, in a slightly worn frock and petticoat. She had blue eyes, a little upturned nose and a long cascade of wavy blonde hair framing the face of an angel. But like an angel she had wings, big wings around her back like a cloak, that would have looked moth-like if they weren't so pale and translucent. She came forward and Dee remembered to close his mouth. As she came closer, he could see the beginning of wrinkles around her eyes and the slight profile of breast and hip that showed she was not really a child. The pointed tops of her ears poked through her hair.

"She is an angel," said Dee, entranced.

"She is one of the people of the forest: one of my Midsummer People. They are being hunted down and killed throughout Europe by the Inquisition and there are very few left. Her husband and her son were caught in Spain and burned at the stake. There was an old woman who was their friend and took care of them and, when she was accused of being a witch, they burned her 'familiar spirits' with her. Madimi fled here, to London. She brings me news of the Inquisition near Madrid. It is from people like Madimi that I have my only information about the Inquisition and about the legends of the world. But she is not an educated woman." Dee looked around again but Madimi had vanished. Colin continued, "I need your library. I need to find our Teacher before Eva of Castile does and we need to make sure that the matter is resolved to the best interests of England. These islands could be the last place for the magic before it is driven out of the world." Colin looked over to the corner where Madimi had been. She waved a shy wave with a shy smile.

Doctor Dee looked over at the child-woman-creature. The widow. "All right," he said, "I'll help you with your refuge. If I learn the way to live forever, that will be good. But I don't want to be a mage in a world with no magic. I'll help you stop her."

Gustavo left them after that, to talk about magician things. He was a swordsman, not a magician. He went to a quiet room near the commons. Paula came with ale and stew from the pot. As she was setting them down, Madimi tugged at Gustavo's sleeve. She had her baby now, clinging to her side, in that strange way that the Midsummer People's children cling.

"Is the other man going to help us then?" she asked him, in her well-spoken Spanish.

For some reason, the voice reminded him of Eva, of his own Eva: not the witch of the Sea People but his lost love. He missed the next thing she said, distracted, far away under the orange trees, between his grandfather's house and the Atlantic Ocean.

She repeated it. "Will things be all right now, Don Gustavo?"

"Yes, mistress," he replied, "Things will be better after this."